RUSTLERS
A JESSIE WEAVER WESTERN ADVENTURE
BOOK 2

William Tresler

Contents

Chapter 1
The Wrong Brand

Jessie Weaver threw back her whiskey and sat the tumbler back down on the bar top with a ringing smack against the alcohol-sodden wood. As she did, her eye caught a movement beside her. A burly, black-mustached man deposited himself on the next bar stool. He caught her eye, and the gleam in it turned her stomach. She tensed.

"Howdy, barkeep," the man said, turning his gaze toward Sam Granger, standing to attention behind the bar counter. "A whiskey for me and another for the lady, here." He turned to face Jessie again, his eyes giving her a good once-over, like a cattle rustler sizing up a calf for branding. "It's on me."

Jessie pressed her lips into a hard line. She promised Tanner and Danny she wouldn't let her mouth get her into trouble again, but this saddle tramp was making it harder than she could have imagined keeping that promise. Thankfully, Sam came to her rescue.

"Beggin' your pardon, sir, but the lady don't take drinks from strangers," he said matter-of-factly, his hands working independently of his mouth as he pulled out a tumbler and poured just one drink.

Jessie watched the man stiffen. He actually seemed to grow an inch taller as his eyes flashed with what was clearly indignation.

Sam, apparently oblivous, wiped up a small spill he'd made and went on. "Ya see, she's the…"

The man cut him short. "I can make sure you lose half your customers, buddy. Or you can just fill my order like I asked ya." His pale blue eyes were steely and piercing.

Jessie gave his enormous frame an observant once-over with her eyes, but for very different reasons than what he'd had for scoping her out.

Sam pushed the man's drink toward him and held up his hands in a show of innocence. "Hey, mister, I'm only tryin' t' give ya fair warnin', is all. You don't got a clue who you're foolin' with, an' I wouldn't want ya smartin' for it."

The man threw back his head and let out a loud, derisive guffaw. Jessie had been thinking of removing herself, but she decided against it, her natural curiosity overcoming her desire to get away from those cold, calculating blue eyes. They were looking at her now, even as their owner addressed Sam.

"Who I'm fooling with? Hell, pardner, this kind of woman, they're all the same. All want the same thing. Attention. That's why they go struttin' around in feller's getup, wearin' guns they couldn't hit the broad side of a barn with, an' drinkin' wild mare's milk. An' I'm right ready t' give this young lady all the attention she'll ever need."

He swung his gaze over to Jessie again. Before it ascended to her face, a stronger desire to put the yellow-bellied skunk in his place had roundly overtaken her desire to flee. She held his gaze as he slipped a clearly well-practiced arm around her waist.

Halfway, he froze, a mist of confusion clouding the brazen arrogance in his eyes. Without a word, Jessie dug the barrel of the LeMat deeper into the man's ribs, taking care to angle it so he could feel the front post sight grating against the bone. Just to erase any doubts he might be having. She noticed his eyes flicker toward his left thigh for the tiniest fraction of a second.

The saloon had gone quiet except for the lazy buzzing of a fat bluebottle slamming itself uselessly against the dusty, sun-drenched, west-facing window of the Hungry Bear. Jessie happily took advantage of his hesitancy.

"Yeah, I reckon that wouldn't be a good idea, mister," she drawled, the laziness in her voice belying the fact that every sense, every nerve, was on high alert. "You know, if you want my advice, I'd tell ya t' start practicin' a straight draw, instead of that clumsy cross-draw. See, you ain't foolin' nobody wearing that firin' iron on your left side now. A blind feller in the dead of night could see you're a right-hander. What with the butt pointin' forward and you drinkin' with your right hand, an' all."

The man hurriedly withdrew his hand from her waist, staggered back from his barstool, and spread both arms out wide, his eyes riveted to the barrel of the pistol. Jessie kept the LeMat trained on him, not moving it a whit to the right or left.

"What kind of females you let into your saloon, mister?" the man yelled at the barkeep, his eyes a gamut of fear, anger, and embarrassment.

Sam shrugged and winked at Jessie. "Ain't got no choice, really, since the boss signed her on as a bouncer 'bout a week ago."

Instantaneously, the whole saloon erupted into roars of laughter, whoops and whistles, and cries of "Well, dogies!" and "I'll be danged!"

The man's face turned a crimson shade of purple. "Dang y'all t' hell!" he ranted, staring at the cowboys and ranchers and saddle tramps who were slapping their palms against their thighs or a table, whichever came first to hand.

Then he turned his pale, mean eyes on Jessie once more. "Better watch your back, ya little hussy. I'll be comin' for ya, mind my words," he snarled as the laughter subsided.

"Is that right?" Jessie replied, coolly re-holstering her pistol. There was little chance the man would draw on her now, not with so many witnesses. Besides, he already knew she had him pegged. It wouldn't be a fair fight.

She looked up into his face again, staring thoughtfully at the enraged twist of his mouth. "Mind givin' me your handle, mister? Just so as I'll know who t' look out for."

The saloon once more burst into gales of merriment, turning the man an even deeper shade of purple and making his veins stand out on his neck.

"I swear on my mother's life, you won't see Gale Bates comin' before you've eaten my bullet," he snapped. Then he turned and stalked out of the saloon, his gait stiff, his back ramrod straight.

Gale Bates, whoever he was, had barely pushed aside the swinging doors of the saloon before Jessie was engulfed in a wave of curious cowhands, most of them leather-skinned and sporting silvering sideburns.

Jessie would rather have forgotten there was a war on, but the scarcity of young men was an unsympathetic reminder. In all the towns she and her brother and friend had passed through on their way from New Mexico Territory to Idaho Territory, they'd noticed the same thing.

"Say, ma'am, Sam ain't kiddin' about ya bein' the bouncer, is he?" a wiry but tough-looking man asked, his gray eyes dancing with private amusement.

"I ain't ma'am. I'm Jessie," she replied flatly. "And Sam ain't kiddin'."

"Lord love ya, ma'am," another voice said, belonging to a ruddy-faced, redheaded, broad-shouldered fellow, his blue eyes sparkling too. "I ain't seen no one take Gale Bates down a peg or two like you just did. He sure had it comin'!"

A smattering of laughter and enthusiastic nods punctuated his declaration.

"I told ya, I ain't ma'am, I'm—" Jessie tried to reiterate, but she was interrupted by the first man.

"Well, Jessie, we'd sure love t' know more about ya. I'm Hank Baumann," he said, sticking out his hand for her to shake.

Jessie obliged him, shrinking internally from having to tell the huddle of admiring strangers anything about herself. "Ain't much t' tell," she muttered, looking down at her empty whiskey glass.

"Can I buy ya a drink, Jessie?" the redhead offered eagerly.

"That's almighty kind of ya, ah..."

"Name's Hamish McGee," the man said, offering his hand.

Jessie shook it. "Reckon I won't make use of that offer, though. Not while I'm on the job." She didn't think it necessary to tell them she had a rule: only two whiskeys a day. She'd seen what drunkenness did to folks, and it had put the fear of God in her.

"Say, Jessie," another man asked, his eyes straying to where they all now knew her LeMats were hidden beneath her dark brown, knee-length leather coat. "I'm figuring Bates was wrong about ya not knowin' how t' use those firin' irons under your jacket."

"Well, I sure as blazes wouldn't have got the bouncer job if I couldn't fire 'em straight, now would I?" Jessie countered dryly.

Laughter rippled through the group once more.

"She sure got ya there, Wally," Hank quipped, giving the slightly squint-eyed questioner a humorous wink.

Wally huffed. "Well, I'd like t' see for myself, if it ain't too much bother for Miss Jessie," he said, a little defensively.

Jessie felt bad for her sarcasm. "Well, all right," she said, rising from the barstool. The crowd before her parted like the Red Sea before Moses, and she walked out of the saloon into the street.

It was a typical frontier town. One single street was bordered on both sides with false-fronted mud-brick and clapboard buildings. A rickety boardwalk ran along the front of most of the buildings. There was no post office, no sheriff's office, and no church. But there were three saloons.

The one she had just stepped out of, the Hungry Bear, was near the end of the long main street.

Jessie cast about for something to shoot at, then noticed a discarded can lying in the alley across the way from the saloon. A mangy looking dog lay not two feet away, its paws twitching as it chased rabbits in its dreams. Planting her feet firmly on the floorboards, Jessie steadied herself, mentally judged the distance and angle, took a deep breath, and held it. In one smooth motion, she pulled the LeMat from its holster on her right hip, raised it, and fired.

The can leaped into the air like a living thing at the same moment the report from the LeMat echoed around the sunbaked, rain-grayed buildings. The dog sprang to its feet with a startled yelp and took off running down the alley, raggedy tail tucked firmly between its legs, without so much as a backward glance over its shoulder.

A shocked silence followed. Jessie quietly slipped the LeMat back into its holster. A face appeared in an upstairs window. A few heads poked out the doors along the street. One man came running out of the general store, his hand on his pistol butt. He stopped, looking confused, as the crowd around Jessie laughed.

"You figured I'd miss, didn't ya, fellas?" Jessie asked rhetorically, folding her arms over her chest.

"I can't buy ya a drink, but I'm sure as hell goin' t' buy ya a coffee," Hamish insisted, taking her elbow and steering her back into the saloon.

Once inside, sipping self-consciously on the coffee she felt it would have been an affront to refuse, Jessie wished

Danny and Tanner would hurry and show their faces. The men were peppering her with questions.

Where did she learn to shoot? What was her last name? Could she rope steer? Brand them? Build a fence? Castrate a calf? Where did she come from? What was she doing here in Buckwheat?

Thankfully, the questions were coming so thick and fast, she could pick what she answered. As far as she was concerned, nobody needed to know where she came from or what she was doing anywhere.

"Hold on a minute, fellers," one curly-haired man piped up, and the barrage died down. "I recollect hearin' stories about a Cattle Kate in New Mexico Territory. Folks said she could ride better than most men, break broncs nobody else could come close to without bein' thrashed, fight off bandits attackin' a stage single-handed."

Jessie tried not to look into their eyes. She didn't want to talk about it, but she didn't know how to tell them so without being rude. She'd already broken her promise to Danny, but she didn't want to break it to such an extreme.

"Word is she rescued a feller who was kidnapped, too. Apache called her White Woman Big Medicine or somethin' like that," the stranger went on.

Eyebrows raised, and a few tut-tuts could be heard. It seemed to Jessie the men were each privately deciding whether they were going to believe such fantastical reports. Hopefully they wouldn't.

"He talkin' about you, Miss Jessie?" Hamish asked, his blue eyes searching her face. "Are you White Woman Big Medicine?"

"Ah, there y'are, Jess!" a familiar and very welcome voice interrupted, saving her from having to make a reply to Hamish's question.

She looked up and smiled gratefully. "Here I are, Dan," she quipped dryly, standing to her feet. She downed the dregs of her coffee and nodded to the men gathered around her. "Sorry, fellas. I got t' go. It's sure been wild." Taking a step toward Danny and trying not to notice the disappointment on her admirers' faces, Jessie turned to look in the barkeep's direction. "You mind if I take a few hours off, Sam?"

"Take all the time ya need, Jess," Sam obliged generously.

Jessie nodded her gratitude, linked her arm into Danny's, and marched him to the swing doors. Grabbing her hat from the coat rack, she couldn't get out fast enough. "What took y'all so long?" she hissed in Danny's ear as they stepped out onto the boardwalk.

"We came as quick as we could," Danny laughed, winking at Tanner, who stood waiting by their horses. "Now unhitch Horace, an' we'll tell ya all about what we learned."

Jessie did as her brother suggested, and soon the three were riding down the main street toward the Bighorn Mountains, capped with white and majestic as they towered up out of the rolling hills that preceded them. "So? You fellas find us a ranch t' work?" Jessie asked impatiently.

"Sure did," Tanner replied, lounging in the saddle as his horse stepped out with strides that effortlessly ate up the ground. "Fella by the name of Baltimore Eustace French."

Jessie rolled her eyes, wondering how much a fellow with a name like that knew about ranching. Still, there wasn't much in a name these days that could give a body an inkling of what the owner might be capable of.

"He's the only one they know of lookin' for more hands. Mr. Crawford said he's only needin' one extra hand, and I wanted us t' keep together, if we could, so I figured we could give Mr. French a try," Danny added. "Here's hopin' there won't be too steep of a price t' pay for it."

Jessie frowned at him quizzically. "Price?" she echoed.

"Seems Mr. French got himself nice an' cozy with the Oglala Sioux around these parts. Married one of their womenfolk," Tanner elaborated on Danny's behalf. "Folks seem t' think he's a little off."

Jessie huffed, turning her attention back to the road that stretched out between Horace's pricked, sandy ears. "I'll wager he's no more *off* than I am," she muttered.

"You're forgettin' there are folks who think you are, too," Danny reminded her with a wink.

"You're forgettin' I can whip your sorry behind if I've a mind to," Jessie retorted, giving him her ornery big sister look.

Danny laughed. "I ain't forgotten. Never you mind," he assured her.

They rode on in silence for a while, each engrossed in their own thoughts. The road became a wagon trail, and the wagon trail split off into a fork when they were about a mile out of Buckwheat.

"Well, I'm hopin' you two know how we get to Mr. French's ranch," Jessie said.

"Sure," Danny replied. "They said take the first right fork, keep on till ya hit Crazy Woman Creek an' follow it all the way up to the Powder River. Mr. French's place is on top of the hill, they said."

Jessie reined Horace to a halt. "Quit lollygaggin' around, Dan," Jessie said in as ominous a voice as she could. "That ain't the name of that creek, no how."

Danny and Tanner both swung their horses around to look at her. Danny was clearly losing the battle against laughing out loud. He tried to talk, but instead he sat in his saddle and shook with suppressed humor.

"If that ain't the name of that creek, then the townsfolk of Buckwheat just straight up lied to our faces," Tanner answered in Danny's stead.

Jessie eyed him for a moment, aware her brother was slowly regaining his composure. Although they did both have a twinkle in their eye, Jessie had known Tanner long enough to tell when he was being honest. He was being honest now. "All right, I'll believe ya," she said, and nudged Horace into a walk again. "They tell you anything else about this rancher we're goin' t' see?""Nah. What we told ya is all we know. Some fellas reckon if we ride for him, we're ridin' for the wrong brand," Tanner answered reflectively.

"Seems kinda fittin'," Jessie said, more to herself than to the others as she let her eyes roam the lush grasslands and patches of forest that covered the rolling hills like a handmade quilt. "Folks is always stickin' the wrong brand on me, anyhow."

Chapter 2
Opportunity

Boston was bustling and noisy as it always was on a July morning, and Richard Hastings, Junior, reveled in the fact he could escape it all in the opulent snuggery of the smoking room of the Somerset Gentlemen's Club. Tapping some ash from his cigar, Richard took a deeply satisfying draw, blowing the smoke up toward the ornately frescoed ceiling. His other hand dropped the newspaper it held into his lap and reached for a glass of port standing on a small, brass side table next to the leather upholstered chair he reclined in.

"Well, well, well! If it isn't Rick Hastings!"

The voice, strident in its excitement, nearly made Hastings drown himself involuntarily in sweet alcohol. He righted the glass spilling nothing and looked up irritably to see who had so rudely disturbed his peace. "Ah, Risling. I should have known it was you," he sighed wearily, not bothering to mask his reticence to entertain the other gentleman, if he could be called that.

James Risling, a staunch abolitionist and Hastings's least favorite member of the Somerset club, deposited himself in the matching leather chair opposite Hastings. He grinned and held out an empty glass that he'd got from who knew where, ostensibly waiting for Hastings to fill it with port from his personal, and rather expensive, bottle. Hastings sighed and obliged.

He would have to put up with Risling's brass-necked behavior or suffer becoming the principal subject of the man's infamous weekly reports to the club chairman, though Hastings preferred to think of them as gossip sessions.

Risling took a sip of the amber liquid in the glass and closed his eyes, apparently rolling the dessert wine around in his mouth to fully appreciate its excellent qualities. Suddenly, his eyes snapped open. "Have you heard what's happening in the Montana Territory?" he asked, his eyes eagerly begging Hastings to answer to the negative.

"Can't say I have," Hastings replied, truthfully. "Although, I'm sure it isn't called the Montana Territory anymore. As I recall, they changed it in favor of Idaho Territory just a few months ago."

Risling waved off his correction. "What's in a name? You know which area I'm referring to, don't you?"

Hastings replied with stony silence, taking a sip of his wine.

"Well, they've found gold in the mountains," Risling announced, his eyes shining with self-importance.

"Gold? That's old news, Risling," Hastings replied, shaking out his newspaper and reading again. Hopefully, the man would take the hint and remove his carcass from the room.

"Grasshopper Creek is *old news*," Risling retorted.

The self-satisfied grin on Risling's face drove Hastings to heights of irritation that made him have to bite back a highly ungentlemanly remark. "Is it now?" he ground out sarcastically instead.

"Indeed," Risling confirmed. "Alder Gulch is all the investors are talking about now. They're saying it's the motherlode. Much bigger than Grasshopper Creek. Folks are streaming there in their thousands as we speak."

Hastings's ears pricked, but he tried not to show any interest, keeping his eyes glued to the black print in front of him, even though he was not taking in a single word he read.

"Trouble is," Risling went on, as Hastings knew he would—the fellow dearly loved the sound of his own voice, and for once, it suited Hastings down to the ground. "The trail isn't what you'd call good traveling. Not much water, terribly rocky in some places. It's making the cost of getting the gold out far too great for most folks."

"That's too bad," Hastings murmured and meant it.

"Exactly what I said," Risling agreed. "But now folks are talking about blazing a trail through the Powder River Basin."

This time, Hastings couldn't hide his interest. "The Powder River Basin?" he echoed incredulously, lifting his eyes from the typeset to scrutinize Risling's face. "You can't be serious." He almost didn't feel irritation at Risling's smug look of one-upmanship when he replied.

"Oh, I'm dead serious," Risling quipped with a wink that Hastings ignored. "The native tribes can't hold a monopoly on the Midwest forever. They'll have to give way to progress at some point or another. May as well be now. Of course, it's sad, but it's also inevitable."

Hastings shook his head dubiously. "It's not as simple as all that. There are treaties protecting them, as well as the fact they know that land better than anyone. I wouldn't send a wagon train through there if you paid me to."

"Well, that's not what the folks down in Montana Territory think," Risling replied smugly, tossing back the rest of his port and holding out his glass for a refill.

Hastings obliged automatically, his mind on more important matters than port at that juncture. He wanted to say, "Idaho," but he held his tongue, instead asking pensively, "Have any wagon trains gone through yet?" It helped to remind himself that one didn't need to like someone in order to get useful information out of them.

"No, but there are a couple of boys planning on it. Someone by the name of Bozeman and, ah, Hurlbut, I think. Rather remarkable names." Risling chuckled and sipped appreciatively on his wine.

"And the military? Are they supporting? Sending troops along?"

Risling leaned forward, his elbows on his knees. "They don't want to get involved, but if you ask me, it's merely a matter of time before there's an attack on the wagons and they're forced to respond. I suppose that'll move things along a little."

Hastings nodded, taking it all in as he dragged thoughtfully on his cigar. "I suppose it will." He gazed past Risling's left ear, staring with unseeing eyes at the heavy red velvet drapes on the floor-to-ceiling window beyond. The Powder River Basin was an enormous piece of real estate, until now guarded by the Lakota, Cheyenne, and Arapahoe nations that used it for their hunting grounds. It was, some said, sacred ground, containing ancient trails that had been used for centuries by the hunter-gatherer forebears of the tribes who now inhabited it.

Hastings cared little about that. The only thing sacred to him was the almighty dollar, and that had been the only reason he'd stayed away from the gold rush to Grasshopper Creek. Too many gold finds were proving a flash in the pan, not worth gambling his hard won cash on.

But, if Risling was right and this Alder Gulch find was lucrative enough to have men blazing new trails to reach it—through deadly Indian-controlled territory, no less—well then, Richard Hastings, Junior, just might be interested.

Not that he would ever concede that to the likes of James Risling, of course. Instead, Hastings drained the dregs of his own port glass and set it down beside the bottle. He carefully folded up his newspaper—making sure not to make new folds in it—rolled it up, and slapped it against his leg. He stubbed out the half-smoked cigar and rose to his feet. "Well Risling, it was topping to see you and have a grand old chinwag, but I'd best be going. Business to attend to, as always. Why don't you finish the port?" Hastings punctuated his farewell with a curt nod and moved away.

"Don't mind if I do," Risling responded, with a grin spreading from ear to ear. "If I didn't know better, I might think Rick Hastings is on his way to do some prospecting." He laughed loudly at his own observation.

Hastings glanced back briefly, responding with a far more hollow laugh. Then he strode between the large, walnut inlaid doors, leaving Risling to regale himself with his own wit. "Except any fool knows there's more money in mining the miners than swirling river gravel around in a pan," he muttered derisively under his breath.

***

The lettering on the door was slightly crude but had clearly been done with great care, despite the inferiority of the materials: *Major John S. Wood.* The battered but brightly polished brass door knocker, shaped in a realistic rendition of a lion's head, teeth bared, nose wrinkled in a ferocious snarl, produced a loud, sharp ringing sound as Hastings rapped it briskly, three times.

"Enter!" a deep, slightly hoarse voice on the other side commanded in response.

Turning the brass doorknob, Hastings pushed at the heavy mahogany door, and it swung open on protesting hinges.

A dark-haired man sat behind a cluttered desk. He looked to be in his mid-thirties but had the air of a man far his senior. His wavy locks were slicked in place with copious amounts of oil and piled up on his head, the fashionable side-parting of the day complimenting the neat, slightly curled mustache that underlined his unremarkable nose and a tiny, almost laughable, goatee that clung to his lower lip.

"Major Wood, I presume," Hastings said, stepping closer and holding out his hand.

The man stood up, the buttons on his coat straining to keep his bulky frame properly encased in the dark blue woolen twill. "At your service, sir," the major barked, vigorously pumping Hastings's hand. "And who might you be?"

Hastings flexed his fingers to restore the circulation in them before he settled into the plush, if slightly tatty, upholstered chair in front of the major's desk. "Richard

Merriweather Hastings, Junior, is the name," he introduced himself. "I trust you've received my latest letter?"

"Hastings, eh?" Wood interjected, his bushy, dark brown brows meeting in concentration. Then he rummaged through some papers on his desk. "Ah, yes," he said, pulling out a crumpled page that Hastings only recognized by his handwriting sprawled across it. "Not sure if you know what you're asking for, Mr. Hastings. The situation isn't what you'd call stable at this point."

Hastings looked down at his shoes. They were dustier than he liked, but thankfully, or hopefully, he wouldn't be around long enough for that to become more than a fleeting irritation. "It's true that the Bozeman and Hurlbut trains have started out on the trail already, isn't it?" he asked, feigning ignorance and sidestepping the major's statement.

"Sure, they have. But they got turned back by Red Cloud's men. I warned them against it, but they wouldn't listen. Set out from Deer Creek Crossing and didn't make it more than a day's travel when they got surrounded by irate Lakota. Sent them right back where they came from. A miracle nobody got killed. It's not worth it, Mr. Hastings. The sooner folks realize that, the better."

Hastings sized up his opposition. Wood surely had orders to stick to the dratted Horse Creek Treaty, signed little over a decade before. He also—if Hastings had accurately sized him up in the few moments since they had met each other—had his own reticence toward engaging the Lakota. Despite his formidable size, Wood struck Hastings as somewhat of a gentle giant, a man far more likely to settle a dispute peaceably than lay down the law by force. No wonder his wasn't a name Hastings had heard before.

Not that it particularly concerned him that the commander of Fort Laramie appeared to be a meek lamb in a land full of wolves. In fact, it suited him splendidly. People who weren't given to looking for trouble rarely found it, even if it was staring them in the face. Hastings remembered the remarks from some soldiers he'd interviewed while pretending to be merely a curious visitor.

Despite his lack of hunger for conflict, Major Wood was known to the men to have an unpredictable temper. He could fly off the handle at the drop of a hat, but not always for no reason. Still, his temper never seemed to solidify into decisive action. One young trooper told Hastings a story of how the nearby ranchers had complained that they were being raided, and Major Wood had sent out men to scout for the hostiles.

After days of searching, they'd been able to find nothing and returned to the fort. Unsaddling their horses, the men, including the trooper who told the tale, had left the animals to roll in the dust of the parade grounds at their leisure.

"We were all in the mess room, enjoying our first decent dinner in three days, when we hear this thundering noise. Me and the others looked at each other. I could tell we were all thinking the same thing. 'What in the blazes? There weren't thunderheads a moment ago.' Next thing, we hear whooping and hollering, and there's dust everywhere. Me and Biggs, here, were the first outside, and what do you think we saw?"

The young soldier had paused for effect, his eyes twinkling with excitement, and Hastings could almost see the images of what had transpired in the next few moments flickering in the young man's eyes. "I'm sure I do not know." Hastings gave him the satisfaction of finishing his own story.

"Well, I'll tell ya," the soldier grinned. "That entire herd of horses went galloping past us. Close enough to reach out and touch them, I swear it. Must've been at least twenty or thirty Indians, driving those horses hard as they could go, screeching and yelling something right fearsome. Before any of us could gather our wits, they were clear out to the hills." He slapped his thigh at this point and shook his head, a dry chuckle emerging from his throat.

"Unbelievable," Hastings remarked. "You fellows get any horses back?"

"Oh, some, but only the weakest nags. Chased their trail for a good solid two days, first light till nightfall, and all we picked up were the stragglers. They left the weak ones behind. Major Wood was madder than an old wet hen, and then some, but there was nothing he or we could do about it. They'd licked us good."

He paused and lowered his voice. "I tell ya, mister, some folks back east—and even some folks 'round here—they think Indians are stupid just 'cause they don't use wheels or build houses or dress or talk like white folks do, but I swear, the more I've seen of them, the more I'm thinking they're a hell of a lot smarter than most of us give them credit for."

Hastings smirked knowingly. "I believe you're right, young fellow. People have forgotten the wise adage, 'Never underestimate your enemy.' However, I believe the thing that's kept the tribes so strong all these years is the fact that they're not soft. They don't tolerate weakness. They don't have time for stragglers. It shows in how they left those weak horses behind. They would not hold on to things that would slow them down. No sentimental nonsense in their minds."

"For a moment there, you had me fooled, mister," the young soldier confessed. "You were sounding an awful lot like an Indian lover."

"Something have not accused me of loving anyone, boy," Hastings replied dryly. "Loving your enemy is for those religious nuts at the mission stations. I've learned you don't have to love your enemy to respect him. But when you lose respect for your enemy, you end up underestimating him, and that's a fatal weakness."

The soldier stared at him, looking a little bewildered.

Hastings patted him on the arm. "Never you mind. You strike me as a fellow who's walking around with his eyes open. One day, you'll understand. Just keep those eyes of yours wide open and don't believe everything you hear."

The young man nodded dumbly, and Hastings rose lithely to his feet, satisfied he had imparted some priceless wisdom for a fair assessment of the situation in and around Fort Laramie.

"Mr. Hastings?" the major's voice broke in on Hastings's musings.

"Hmmm… Yes," Hastings said unthinkingly, getting up from the chair. "I suppose you're right, Major. It's just not worth riling up the Indians. Thank you so much for your time and your honest assessment of the situation. You and your men have been most helpful."

Major Wood waved off Hastings's thanks. "Any time you're in a pickle, Mr. Hastings, you come straight to me. I'll help you out any way I can."

"I'm sure you will, Major. I'm sure you will."

Chapter 3
Frenchie

Mr. Baltimore Eustace French wasn't exactly what Jessie had been expecting, which was a refreshing change for her since things were usually the other way round when she met folks she didn't know. It began with Mr. French's house.

Far from the sprawling rancher's house cutting a swaggering figure on a nearly bare hillside, Mr. French's house was best described as a large cabin, Jessie thought, nestled cozily in a cluster of pine and cottonwoods.

Mr. French himself was outside when they arrived, chopping wood for his woodpile. His red-checkered sleeves were rolled up to his elbows, and his deeply tanned, leathery face was partly concealed by a luxurious, salt-and-pepper beard. His startling green eyes were calm and friendly as he raised his hat in greeting to the three strangers riding onto his farm.

"Well, howdy!" he called out, dropping his axe and brushing his hands off on his denim overalls as he stepped closer. "You folks must be lookin' for me. Nobody rides through here unless someone gave 'em directions." He laughed happily at his own joke, his eyes twinkling.

"Well, if you're Baltimore Eustace French yeah, we're lookin' for you," Tanner said, his own sun-weathered face creasing into a smile.

"The one and only," Mr. French shot back without missing a beat. "But you can call me Frenchie. Most folks do. The white folks, at least. My Sioux friends call me Mato Istime. Means sleeping bear." He laughed again.

"Reckon I'll stick with Frenchie since I can't hardly go around callin' a fella Sleepin' Bear." Danny said, dismounting and offering their new acquaintance his hand. "My name's Danny Weaver. And this here's my friend Tanner Nugent and my sister, Jessie Weaver." He gestured to each as he introduced them.

Jessie waited for the inevitable incredulous exclamation, *Your sister? Oh, hell! For a moment, I thought that was a fella!* But it never came.

Instead, Frenchie stepped toward her, where she still lounged in the saddle and held out his hand. "It's a real pleasure t' meet ya, Jessie," he said in exactly the same tone and with the same expression he used to greet Tanner and Danny before her.

Jessie felt the firm, rough grasp of his work-calloused hand and instantly decided she liked Frenchie. "You mind my askin' how come the Sioux call ya Sleepin' Bear?" she blurted, without thinking.

Frenchie chuckled. "Well, truth be told, it's my wife started it. See, I get awful ornery when I'm wakened in the mornin'. Like a bear wakin' up from his winter sleep, she always says." He chuckled again. "I'll own I never took much of a likin' to the name at first, but it grew on me." He looked around at the two men, his eyes still friendly. "What brings you folks out here, then?"

"We heard you were lookin' for hands," Tanner explained. "Fella named Crawford said you were a mite short."

"Crawford, eh?" Frenchie said, a shadow flitting across his eyes. It was gone quicker than it came, though. "Well, he sure hit the nail on the head. I've been short for a while. Can't seem t' have fellers stay for more than a couple weeks lately. I sure hope y'all are fixin' t' stay permanent, like. I can sure do with the help." He stroked his bushy beard hopefully.

Jessie caught Tanner's eye and then Danny's. She nodded. She knew why the men had left. They didn't like working for a white man who had set up house with a woman from a native tribe. Like as not, they didn't even acknowledge Frenchie's marriage. She glanced around, curious to see the other half of the French union. As if reading her mind, Frenchie called out over his shoulder.

"Tasha! Come on out. There're some folks here t' meet ya."

Moments later, a tall, slender woman emerged from the shadowy interior of the house. She was clad in a long, light brown deerskin tunic that went to her ankles. Fringes adorned the hem and the long, wide sleeves and an intricate pattern of blue, white, and red beads festooned the shoulders. A collar and cuffs of soft, brown rabbit fur completed the garment.

The woman's hair was plaited into two long braids, entwined with red rawhide that was then used to bind the ends. Her neck was long and elegant, her skin a rich caramel brown and glowing with health, her steps fluid and full of ease and grace, and her eyes as she came to stand beside her husband were deep, liquid brown, soulful yet self-contained.

Jessie couldn't remember ever seeing such a beautiful woman. It almost made her want to wear dresses again, if they looked like that. If she could look like that. So feminine and yet so strong.

"This here is Tasha, my wife, known to her Sioux folks as Iyagkececa Tahca, Runs Like a Deer." He gazed at her lovingly.

"Mighty pleased t' meet ya, ma'am," Danny said, stepping forward and holding out his hand. "Name's Danny Weaver, and this is my sister, Jessie, an' my friend Tanner Nugent."

"You are welcome," Tasha said, her eyes passing calmly from one to the other. There was no bowing, no fluttering eyelashes, no flushing cheeks or feigned smiles. Just simple, confident acknowledgement and acceptance. Jessie had the distinct impression that Tasha already knew, from one glance, who they were and that she could trust them.

"These three came out here offerin' their services, love," Frenchie informed his wife. "I'll be takin' 'em down to Fort Laramie, so as they can meet Mr. Brookes."

Tasha nodded. "Tomorrow. Now we eat." She smiled and motioned to her guests to come inside the cabin.

The French house was snug and homely. Everywhere, there were buffalo robes and decorations of feathered beadwork. An elaborately carved sideboard housed a collection of wood-framed, grainy photographs of Frenchie, Tasha, and some other people unfamiliar to Jessie. Baskets sat beside earthenware on the shelves and decorated the walls and floor. The scent of pine needles filled the room as the smoke curled up from some green leaves slowly burning in an abalone shell.

In the sunniest corner of the room, a boy of about five years old sat on a pile of buffalo robes and cradled a baby in his arms, singing softly while he rocked back and forth. He looked up as Jessie and her friends entered, and his innocent features broke into a broad smile. His eyes shone golden brown in a face darker than Frenchie's but lighter than Tasha's, and his black, curly hair hung around his shoulders.

"Chaske," Frenchie said, "say howdy to our guests."

"Howdy!" the little boy obliged happily, not stopping his rocking motion. "You gonna work for my pa?"

Jessie smiled and nodded. "I sure hope we are," she replied.

Chaske's grin broadened. "And can you help Mama with Macawi so I can play in the woods more?" He nodded toward the babe in his lap.

A sharp clucking sound prevented Jessie from replying, and Chaske looked guiltily at his mother standing behind Jessie.

"Mind your manners, Chaske," she said, her tone disapproving but clearly a reprimand given in love.

Unbidden, a memory flashed through Jessie's mind of her own mother. Mama had used the same tone on her, firm yet gentle. A deep longing filled her, but she brushed it aside.

"I reckon your pa'll be keeping me plenty busy takin' care of his beeves, but if I get the time, I sure will take care of, ah…" she hesitated.

"Macawi," Chaske helped her out. "Means girl coyote. When she was born, there was a coyote howlin' outside the window. I howled with him." He patted his chest proudly. Baby Macawi stirred in her sleep and made a few small, squeaking sounds.

"She knows we speak of her," Tasha said, stepping forward and taking the child from her son's arms. "Chaske, you help Papa with the food. I'll take care of Macawi."

"Ha, Ina," the boy said, surrendering his sister and scurrying to his father's side.

"Make yourselves comfortable, folks," Frenchie invited them amicably. "Dinner'll be served soon."

It was, and it was, a meal the like of which Jessie had never tasted. It was simple enough—deer meat stewed with corn, beans, and squash—but the flavors were so robust and the seasoning so delicate that it left Jessie's mouth watering and every fiber in her body crying out for more.

"We grow our own greens out back," Frenchie told his guests between mouthfuls. "The deer was a little long in the tooth, but Tasha cooked him up good and tender like she always does." He smiled at his wife again, and she blushed.

Jessie couldn't help noting that nothing but her husband's words of adoration could make Tasha anything less than boldly confident. She resolved to take a leaf or two out of the elegant yet fierce Lakota woman's book before her time at the French ranch was over.

The conversation around the table hummed along pleasantly when an insistent knocking at the door intruded on their domestic bliss.

Frenchie's head whipped up. "What in tarnation?" he muttered, wiping his mouth with a table napkin as he rose to his feet. He opened the door of the cabin and there stood a cowhand, a worried expression creasing his face and darkening his eyes. "Wally?"

Wally stepped inside. Jessie remembered him as one man from the Hungry Bear Saloon. The one who'd asked her to display her shooting abilities. He didn't seem surprised to see them, his mind clearly more occupied with an issue of much greater concern than a few new cowhands in his boss's front room.

"Beggin' pardon, boss," Wally said, twisting his hat in his hands. "I got some bad news that can't stand waitin' till later."

"Well, spit it out, Wally," Frenchie urged him, waving him to a chair in the same moment.

Wally sat down heavily and kept twisting his hat. "I rounded up the herd, like ya told me, t' cut out the oxen meant for sellin', an' when I counted 'em there was a bunch missin'."

Frenchie's head snapped back, surprise and disbelief written all over his face. "A bunch missin'?" he repeated, as if he didn't understand the words. "How many is a bunch?"

Wally twisted his hat even harder. "Seems like around fifty, boss," he said, his voice tight with tension.

"Fifty!" Frenchie's head hung forward on his neck, his eyes wide. Then he shook it. "No, can't be that many. That's a tenth of my herd."

"I counted twice, boss," Wally assured him, his eyes sad and fearful at the same time.

Frenchie put his hands on his hips and drew himself up as he inhaled a long, shaky breath. He let it out again in a whoosh and turned to face his new employees. "Hey, folks, this ain't the way I wanted it, but I'm goin' t' have t' leave y'all here while I go look for my stock. You take your time and finish up dinner, now. I'll be back directly."

"Not at all, Mr. Frenchie, sir," Tanner said calmly, rising from his seat at the low table. "Me an' my team, we'll join ya. May as well get a feel for the place before we start work tomorrow, and I reckon y'all can do with a few extra pairs of eyes, anyhow."

Frenchie stared at Tanner for a moment in disbelief, then shifted his gaze to Danny and Jessie. "You sure about that? You don't want t' settle in first?"

Danny shook his head. "We're here now. May as well make ourselves useful," he supported Tanner's statement.

Deep gratitude filled Frenchie's face. "Well, you folks sure know how t' make a feller believe there's still good in the world." He hurried out the door, gesturing for them to follow.

Jessie wondered what had made Frenchie stop believing that. She had little time to think about it, though. Frenchie quickly strode out to the corrals behind his house and counted the cattle enclosed there while Jessie and the others helped Wally keep them from mingling around too much.

"Forty-eight missin'," Frenchie said at last, a worried frown clouding a face that Jessie had thought was the most jovial and friendly she could ever remember seeing. "You folks mind if we scour the range a little? Till night falls?"

Tanner, Danny, and Jessie nodded their agreement in unison.

Frenchie hurriedly caught and saddled a horse. He clambered into the leathers and sat facing them. "Tanner, you come with me. Jessie an' Danny, you folks ride with Wally. That way, we'll get more ground covered."

Within moments, they were off, riding into the slowly fading late afternoon sunshine. For three hours they rode, Wally explaining to Jessie and Danny where the mutually agreed borders of the ranch were and pointing out the cattle's favorite haunts for grazing, watering, and resting.

It was beautiful country: rolling hills, majestic rocky outcrops, tumbling, gurgling streams, and lazy, winding creeks, all covered in a luxurious carpet of prairie grass and a dizzying variety of trees and shrubs. Jessie didn't know the names of half of them. Not that she pondered that much. At the moment, she was far too preoccupied with searching for the missing cattle.

The hours of searching, though, proved to be entirely fruitless. As the last rays of light hastened to join an already absent sun beyond the horizon, five tired riders dismounted and unsaddled their horses, traipsing dispiritedly back into the house.

"I can't make head nor tail of it," Frenchie sighed, sinking down onto a cot covered with a large bearskin rug. He combed his fingers absentmindedly through the thick brown fur. "Who would take so many cows at once?"

"When I was out roundin' up the herd the first time, boss, I saw three riders from a distance, lookin' like they were in an almighty big hurry, but I was focused on my work, so I didn't think nothin' of it. After, when I counted them beeves, I wished I'd taken a closer look at 'em." His eyes mirrored the regret in his voice.

Frenchie gave him a sorrowful look. "Reckon it's better you didn't, Wally. If it was them three fellers who rustled our cows, who knows what they might have done to ya for catchin' 'em red-handed."

"You had any problems before, Mr. Frenchie?" Danny asked cautiously.

Frenchie shook his head. "Me and the Sioux, Tasha's people, we have us a real good understandin'. I've always let 'em take a cow or two for meat if they're hungry and game is scarce. Sort of payment for them keepin' the Cheyenne and the Arapahoe off my back, too. Now and again, there's a couple cows run off by white rustlers, but they're also few an' far between. Most of the time, my boys catch 'em before they can make off with too much beef. This is the first time I've been hit so hard."

"You still have enough t' take down t' Fort Laramie?" Tanner asked.

Frenchie nodded, straightening up a little, as if trying to strengthen himself. "I got a good passel. Strange as it seems, they left most of those. Took the cows with calves. That's how I know it ain't Sioux that took 'em. Not any of the tribes, matter of fact. They've got the smarts t' take the ones that's the least trouble. That's what I can't figure out, no how. Who in tarnation would take nursin' cows, an' why?"

He looked up searchingly at his employees, who stood around him, arms folded, brows furrowed with worry and concentration. Nobody had an answer to his question. Jessie felt a shiver run down her spine. There was more to this than met the eye, she felt sure, but what exactly was going on was still a mystery.

"We'll ride out at first light," Frenchie said, his voice tired but his tone resolute. "It's at least a week's drive down t' the fort if we drive 'em hard." He gave them an apologetic look. "If y'all still are keen on ridin' for the BEF brand, that is."

"Sure, we are," Jessie butted in before Tanner or Danny could reply. She'd found folks she could stand being around for more than a few hours, and she didn't want to risk having to leave there. With a don't-you-dare-say-no glare in her eye, she held Tanner's gaze.

He smiled. "Your problems are our problems now, Frenchie," he said, a strange twinkle in his eye.

Chapter 4
Strangers

Fort Laramie was as much of a surprise to Jessie as her meeting with Frenchie had been. The forts she had been familiar with in New Mexico Territory had been small pokey constructions, surrounded by high walls of either pine tree trunks or adobe or a mixture of the two. They invariably boasted guard towers on two corners and housed only troops and horses.

Not so at Fort Laramie.

The first surprise was that there was no wall around the fort at all. The second was that it was as big as a small town, and almost as bustling. Built on a raised section of earth, partly surrounded by an oxbow of what Frenchie called the Laramie River, the fort sprawled over a large portion of land.

At the center, long, whitewashed barracks surrounded a dusty, flat area, at one end of which stood three cannons. Frenchie said that was the parade ground. Beyond the cannons stood a double-story building with a long balcony across each story and outside stairs on either end going up to the second floor.

In all directions, the same style of square, whitewashed adobe buildings littered the surrounding hillsides, along with huddles of circled wagon trains and clutches of tipis, from which drifting blue wood smoke rose along with the sound of laughing, shouting children and barking dogs.

Within the compound itself, some soldiers were giving their horses a roll in the dirt of the parade ground. A few more horses stood three-legged under the trees at another end and switched their tails lazily.

As Jessie's party approached the double-story building, which Frenchie referred to as "Old Bedlam, where the bachelor soldiers live," a roar of male laughter escaped the sash windows and rolled toward them across the dusty, hard-packed earth.

"Look over there, Jessie," Frenchie said, pointing to a small huddle of figures in the shade of a nearby house's porch awning.

Jessie squinted against the glare of sunlight reflected from the pale earth and the whitewashed buildings. "I'm lookin'."

"Maybe it'll be best for ya t' join those ladies while we're inside talkin' to the fellers."

Jessie stopped dead in her tracks. She squinted again. Yes, they were indeed ladies. Dressed in lace and frills and ribbons and sipping from what appeared to be dainty cups. "There's womenfolk here?" she asked incredulously.

"There sure enough are," Frenchie responded cheerfully. "An' young'uns too. Most all the married officers here brung their families along with 'em."

Jessie stood still for a moment, taking this in. Then she walked resolutely and swiftly toward Old Bedlam. The men hurried to catch up with her.

"Maybe Frenchie's onto somethin', Jess," Tanner said, sounding a trifle nervous. "I reckon the fellas in there ain't used t' womenfolk in their quarters."

Jessie didn't slow her pace or even glance at him. "Well they'll just have t' get used to it in a hurry, won't they? I'm part of this team, an' I ain't sittin' outside like a kid while the grownups take care of business."

Out of the corner of her eye, she could see Tanner and Danny exchange a glance. Then Tanner shrugged, and they reached the steps of Old Bedlam's porch. Another gale of uproarious laughter swept over them as they did. Frenchie tapped on the shoulder of a man standing in the doorway. The man turned around, his face still crimson and creased up with hilarity.

Frenchie raised his hat in greeting. "Howdy, soldier," he said affably. "Anybody round here know where we can find Lieutenant Waters?"

The soldier swallowed his laughter, then nodded. "Ah, sure, sir. Last I heard, he was over at the watering hole. I can take you folks there, if you'd like."

"Much obliged," Frenchie accepted.

Jessie couldn't help asking, "What's going on in there?" as yet another round of laughter burst through the open double doors.

The soldier grinned. "Our theatrical society is rehearsing a play," he replied to Jessie's surprise. "I'm the tuba player, and our band will play music to go with it. They're letting us watch first so we don't lose our composure when we perform the piece. And rightly so. It's quite hilarious! You folks are welcome to watch, if you'd like."

Jessie peered inside the building. The men there were all well dressed, their hands encased in white gloves, their boots shining like mirrors to rival the buttons on their perfectly pressed double-breasted jackets. Far from feeling like she was looking at a gathering of hardened soldiers in a frontier fort, beset by all the dangers and difficulties of the harsh and unforgiving Midwest, Jessie felt she might as well have magically stepped into the town hall of a large eastern city in the heart of so-called civilization.

She backed away, thankful to hear Frenchie turn down the soldier's offer.

"I reckon we'll just see the lieutenant and be on our way," Frenchie said firmly, without losing his friendly tone.

The soldier nodded. "Very well, sir, if you'll just follow me."

He led them to a building close to Old Bedlam where a handful of what appeared to be officers were peacefully reading newspapers and sipping on amber liquid in short, fat glasses. A long, mahogany bar lined one wall, the glass, mirror-backed shelves behind it stocked to the roof with shiny bottles with elaborate labels on them.

At a table near the door, some soldiers were playing poker, using matches instead of money to gamble with.

As they entered, the soldiers looked up. They scanned the group of civilians cursorily, but one fellow's brows rose almost up to his hairline as his eyes rested on Jessie. He gripped the arm of the man beside him.

"Hey, Wilson," he hissed, loudly enough for everyone to hear. "I believe there's a real live Cattle Kate walking through the door."

The man named Wilson looked up eagerly, a smirk already forming on his clean-shaven face. "Well, hello there!" he exclaimed. Every head that hadn't already been looking was now turned toward Jessie. "May I ask you a question, ma'am? You are a ma'am, right?"

"No," Jessie replied flatly. "I ain't ma'am, I'm Jessie."

"Well, Jessie, perhaps you can answer a question that I've never been able to answer myself. Whatever makes a woman in her right mind wear men's clothing?"

A hush fell on the room, broken only by a few whispers and titters. Jessie eyed the man, her impassive mask firmly in place. She wouldn't let him or anyone else see how riled she was. Wouldn't give them the satisfaction.

Slowly and deliberately, she tilted her head to one side, looked Wilson up and down and then stated blithely, "I'd like t' see *you* ropin' steers and brandin' calves in that fancy dude's getup of yours, mister, never mind a ball gown an' high heels."

This time, the hush was complete. Wilson's face reddened as his smirk disappeared like mist on the prairie when the sun rises. A few of his companions couldn't hold their laughter for long, though, but Jessie only heard their explosive snorts and splutters as she turned away from them to face their escort.

She opened her mouth to speak, but Tanner's deep bass cut her short.

"If ya don't see that lieutenant around here, we'd just as soon get out of here," he said crisply, his eyes blazing.

"He's right over there." The soldier pointed to a corner of the room where a tall man sat in a booth. The man's aquiline nose, on which perched a pair of round spectacles, was buried in a newspaper.

Tanner nodded tersely and marched over toward the officer. Frenchie, who had been staring at Jessie with his mouth open, promptly snapped it shut and hurried after Tanner. Danny took Jessie's elbow and, giving her a conspiratorial wink, ushered her across the room, away from the gaggle of greenhorns parading as soldiers.

Parading was the only word Jessie could find to describe what they were doing. She couldn't imagine any of those poor sods surviving a confrontation with the native inhabitants of the wilderness they were floating their little party boat in.

Angrily, she thrust any thought of them aside and focused on the purpose for their visit: to meet the man responsible for buying oxen from the ranchers around Fort Laramie and then selling them to the emigrants headed to Oregon, California, Santa Fe, Mexico, and who knew where else.

Their escort had hurried ahead of Tanner and now came to a ragged halt in front of the lieutenant. Clicking his heels together, he saluted. "Begging your pardon, Lieutenant Waters, but there are some civilians here to see you."

The newspaper lowered, and a pair of cold blue eyes stared at them over the round, wire-rimmed spectacles. As soon as they rested on Frenchie, they defrosted slightly and the lieutenant folded the newspaper.

"Ah, Frenchie," he said, in a decidedly British accent. "Brought some more stock for me, have you? Splendid. I was wondering if you'd be able to deliver."

"I was wonderin' that myself," Frenchie replied grimly under his breath as he removed his hat.

"Do sit down and introduce me to your friends," Lieutenant Waters said, patting the seat beside him.

Frenchie obeyed and motioned to Jessie and the others to follow suit. They did, scooting into the long, leather upholstered seat on the other side of the booth. "These here are my new hands, Waters," he said matter-of-factly. "Danny Weaver, his sister, Jessie, and Tanner Nugent. They'll be drivin' my herds in from here on out. Just so you know they ain't rustlers."

Lieutenant Waters gave a short, mirthless laugh. "So, Frenchie, do I assume correctly that you're having more trouble than usual with stock theft?"

"I sure enough am," Frenchie conceded gloomily. "Matter of fact, I was fixin' t' ask ya if the other ranchers are havin' troubles, too."

"They are, indeed, old chap," Waters informed him. "Gale Bates and Gill Crawford both reported a steep increase in cattle theft this last week. If I'm not mistaken, they had thirty or forty head stolen. Each. Quite irate, they were. Telling me it's got to be the local tribes' stealing."

Frenchie frowned and rubbed his beard. "They got any proof?" he asked.

"Proof? Why? What proof do they need? It's common knowledge, isn't it?" Waters took a sip of his bourbon.

Jessie resisted the urge to snatch it from him and throw it in his face.

"No, it ain't." It was clear to Jessie that Frenchie was fighting his own battle with his temper. "We ain't had trouble like that with the Sioux, nor any of the other nations hereabouts. You know I got a good relationship with 'em, me bein' kin an' all."

"Hmm… Yes, I know about that. Bates knows too. He says there are renegades responsible, and he's itching to go flush them out. Says they're taking chances because they know you won't do anything about it."

Jessie couldn't tell if Waters was agreeing with the Bates fellow or not. But something else was bothering her. She knew that name. Bates. Gale Bates. For a moment, she stared at the amber liquid in the glass. Then it hit her.

The arrogant, groping skunk in the Hungry Bear Saloon down in Buckwheat. She looked closer at Waters, trying to read his eyes, facial expression, anything that would give her a clue about which way he was leaning.

"All Gale Bates is gonna flush out is a heap of trouble. He knows he's t' come t' me if'n there are any shenanigans with the locals. He knows I got Red Cloud's ear." Frenchie was clearly losing the battle against his temper.

Waters shrugged passively. "Now, now, don't shoot the messenger, Frenchie," he said blithely. "I'm only relaying what I've been told by your fellow cattlemen."

"Well, I reckon we'd better do some investigatin'. Who's t' say it wasn't white folks took all our cows? I ain't never seen a Sioux take nursin' cows an' their calves. Too much hassle t'…"

"You'd better keep your voice down, Frenchie," Waters interrupted, his eyes freezing over suddenly. "Wouldn't want you becoming a target now."

Frenchie's eyes flashed. "A target? Of what? Who?"

"Just keep your head and your voice down, old boy, and let things run their course," Waters said, taking another sip of his bourbon.

Jessie glanced at Tanner. He caught her eye and raised his eyebrows ever so slightly. She knew he was thinking the same thing she was. Things were not quite on the up and up around here.

It was just as well they had come in to ride for Frenchie when they had. Looked like he needed all the help he could get, in more ways than one.

Frenchie took a deep breath. "Well," he said, apparently deciding to let the matter rest for the moment. "I brought in those twenty head of oxen I said I'd bring. Dang near didn't have enough t' fill the order, but there they are." He pushed forward the bill of receipt the soldiers had given him when they delivered the cattle.

Waters took it and scrutinized it silently. Then he took out a billfold and counted out the crisp fifty dollar notes. He handed them to Frenchie.

"Don't you worry about anything at all, Frenchie. We'll take care of you and your family, whatever happens." He held out his hand and Frenchie shook it, though Jessie could see the lieutenant's words still bothered him.

They left after that, first stopping at the trading post outside the fort for some supplies, then heading back on the trail bound for Crazy Woman Canyon. It was a long, silent four days' ride.

Frenchie brooded most of the way, and Jessie, Tanner, and Danny didn't have the heart to make any light conversation. Jessie turned the words she had heard over in her mind again and again. No matter which way she looked at it, there was something less than above board going on.

She hadn't been able to come to any conclusions, though, by the time they reached the French ranch. Other than she was determined to stick around and do whatever she could to help one of the kindest, friendliest men she'd had the pleasure of meeting.

As they rode into the cluster of small buildings that was Frenchie's homestead, a horseman entered the clearing from the other side. He rode jauntily, Jessie thought, his sorrel, white-faced horse champing at the bit for no apparent reason, his hat perched rakishly on his head. He seemed to view the world with a sort of superior disdain coloring his green-gray eyes. His black mustache twitched when he rode up to them and saw Jessie.

"Say, boss," he said to Frenchie. "These are the new hands Wally was talkin' about?"

"They surely are," Frenchie replied shortly as he dismounted. "Danny, Tanner, Jessie, this here's Rafe. The only other hand I got besides the three of you, an' Wally."

Jessie caught Danny's eye. He had a strange look on his face. Not that anyone who didn't know him well would have noticed. Jessie, though, could tell his features were unusually stiff and guarded.

"Pleasure," Rafe said, his eyes raking her from head to toe. Jessie glared back, almost wanting him to say something so she could put him in his place, but Frenchie, in the middle of unsaddling his horse, spoke, ending any chance of that happening.

"Reckon Wally told ya about the cows that's stolen, did he?"

"Sure did." Rafe dismounted and threw his horse's reins around the hitching rail. "Cryin' shame. The herd was comin' along real good." His tone didn't seem to match his words.

Something about what he said, as well as the way he said it, struck Jessie as odd, but she couldn't put her finger on what it was.

"Yeah. Waters says the other ranchers are sufferin' too. They reckon it's the Sioux takin' 'em. What's your thinkin'?" Frenchie wasn't looking at Rafe. He was leading his horse away to the corrals out back of the cabin.

Jessie felt the tension in the air thicken immediately.

"I figure that's the most likely," Rafe replied, far too coolly, Jessie thought.

"Me, I wouldn't jump to conclusions so quick," Tanner cut in. "I'm rememberin' what Wally said about white fellas he saw when he was roundin' up the beeves to take 'em down t' Fort Laramie."

Rafe's eyes slid over to Tanner. "Likely just fellers ridin' through. The Indians ain't the only ones as uses these trails." He paused. "Besides, Wally's gettin' a little long in the tooth. Likely he was just imaginin' things."

Danny coughed, seeming to have something stuck in his throat. Tanner slapped him on the back, but we waved off his help and smiled sheepishly. "I'm all right," he said. "Just a little spittle gone down the wrong way."

Jessie could tell something far worse had caused his discomfort.

It was only later that evening, as they were settling down in the two-room bunkhouse, the three of them shared that he spoke up.

"Tanner. Jessie," he said. "I got t' tell y'all somethin'."

The tone of his voice made both of them stop what they were doing and sit down to face him. The light of the kerosene lamps glowed yellow on his face and cast long shadows behind all three of them.

"We're listenin', Danny," Jessie whispered.

"I also saw fellas out on the range while we were searchin' for the missin' cows the other night. Two of 'em, ridin' together." He paused, and Jessie and Tanner exchanged a glance. "Didn't think nothin' of it until now." He paused again, seeming afraid to continue as he glanced fitfully at each of the windows and cleared his throat.

"What made ya think somethin' of it, Danny?" Tanner asked.

In a whisper Jessie could barely hear, her brother said, "I could be wrong. I sure hope I'm wrong, but I could've sworn one of 'em looked just like that Wilson feller who rankled you at the fort, Jessie."

Jessie took in this information silently. Something told her Danny wasn't done.

"An' I'm pretty sure the other one was this feller Rafe we just met tonight."

Chapter 5
Making Friends

The next few days were almost normal, except that their formerly jovial employer was as jumpy as a cat on a hot tin roof. His smile was absent, and his brow continually furrowed with deep, pensive lines.

The work turned out to be too little for all three of Jessie's posse, so she decided on the third day they were there to do good on her promise to young Chaske. She'd already discussed her idea with Tanner and Danny the night before, so they simply shared a smile when she announced after breakfast that she'd like to spend some time with Tasha if that was okay with the boss.

Frenchie looked a little nonplussed, but Danny assured him there wasn't enough work to go around that day anyway.

"An' I surely don't mean no disrespect, Mr. Frenchie, but I reckon it'll do ya good t' spend a little time with yer tyke. Let us young bachelor fellas worry about the ranch for a day." He gave Frenchie a wink.

The older man looked around the table. Rafe didn't seem interested in the conversation at all. He was still tucking into an extra helping of eggs. Wally nodded slowly, a sage, fatherly expression on his scrawny features. Chaske stared wide-eyed at his father, a smile dawning gradually on his flushed, hopeful face.

"Jessie speaks truly," Tasha said in her clear, musical tones. "Worry is like mold in the bones. Laughter is the wind that will blow it away."

Frenchie looked at his son. His face relaxed. "Reckon I'd be a fool t' turn y'all down," he chuckled, the faintest glimmer of the old twinkle returning to his eye.

Jessie felt grateful he'd relented. She wanted to spend some time with Tasha and felt guilty doing it any other day.

When the menfolk had left, she took care of the washing up. Tasha took care of baby Macawi. Neither took very long. With the baby fed, cleaned, and sleeping on a buffalo robe near the woodstove, Tasha poured them each a cup of herbal tea and motioned to Jessie to sit.

"You wish to speak to me," she said, settling down beside her baby.

Jessie's eyes widened and her jaw dropped. Then she snapped it shut.

Of course. She had forgotten how the people of the land seemed to see beyond the faces of others, know their intentions before they spoke them. She took a seat opposite Tasha on another buffalo-robed chair.

Jessie pondered what it was she wanted to know. There were so many questions bustling about in her mind, each one vying for first place in the queue. Finally, she settled on one close to home. It helped to know who people were if a body was going to help them sort out their troubles.

"Tell me your story," she whispered. "You an' Frenchie. How'd you two end up together?"

Tasha smiled. "You think it strange for a white man to marry a Sioux woman, yes?" There was laughter in her voice.

Jessie flushed. "Not so strange as some folks think it is. Besides, there's a heap of folks thinks I'm strange too."

"You would marry a Sioux man?"

The question was unexpected. Jessie flinched, an image of Taza flitting before her mind's eye for a moment. Then she quickly composed herself. "Sure, if I was the marryin' kind to begin with," she said, a little more stiffly than she wanted to.

Tasha's smile softened. "I see you," she said simply.

A breathless silence hung over them for a while. Then Tasha spoke, a faraway look in her eyes, her face dreamy.

"Frenchie came to this land when I was a young girl," she said. "I was not more than twelve summers. He was a trapper. Some called him a mountain man. For many summers, he trapped animals, skinned them, and cured their skins. At first, my people were afraid of him because of his white skin, but some of us were curious. Especially the children. Especially my brothers, Anoki and Kohana."

She chuckled at the memory.

"We watched him make his house, like this one." She gestured about the room. "Only smaller. We watched him play his harmonica, wondering how he could pull those strange sounds out of the shiny little box. One day, Anoki went to take the shiny box while he was away, but he came back and caught us. We thought he would chase us off, shoot at us, yell at us like the other Wasi'chu did. Frenchie did not. He let us blow wind into his harmonica and make the sounds. After that, all the village children wanted to try."

Tasha chuckled again. She took a sip of her tea, apparently savoring the pungent herbal flavors for a while. Then again, she might just as well have been savoring the memories of her childhood.

"Frenchie became a part of our village then, except that he did not move when we moved. Also, he went away every time during ptanyetu, the changeable time, when the leaves changed color and fell from the trees. He went to the land where the sun rises to sell his furs. But every time, he came back. The summers passed, and I grew into a woman. Each wetu, the sun time, when the snows melted, I looked forward more eagerly to see the smoke rising from his wooden lodge." She paused, her cheeks coloring.

"Ya don't have t' tell me everything," Jessie hastened to assure her. Tasha blinked at her in surprise. "Unless ya want to," Jessie added, a deep sense of honor growing in her core.

"On the seventh wetu, when he came back, he had a ring for me. This one." Tasha pointed to the fine silver ring on her third finger. In the middle of it sat a small emerald in the shape of a teardrop. "The stone's color was just like his eyes. He told me he would cry like that teardrop if I would not agree to be his wife. That summer, my people call it bloketu, potato time, we were married."

Baby Macawi whimpered in her sleep, and Tasha turned her attention to the child for a while.

"Did you stay in the cabin?" Jessie asked. "I reckon your folks wouldn't like leavin' ya alone with the trapper while they moved off t' other huntin' grounds."

Tasha shook her head as she caressed her sleeping daughter's face. "My father made him join the tribe for a time. Until Chaske was born. Frenchie did not like to move about with his children still young. He said it is not the way of his people. He asked my father to let us stay in one place. To let us make a home like his cabin, where he would grow cows and oxen and sell them to the settlers going over the mountains to the new land. My father agreed."

Jessie shook her head. "That sure was big of your pa," she breathed.

"Yes. My father, Wambleeska is his name—this means white eagle in your language—he is much respected by my people, just like the eagle who flies far above the earth and sees things that those below do not see."

"I reckon that would make him a good chief," Jessie said, wondering what it would be like to speak to this White Eagle.

"He is not chief." Tasha smiled gently. "Our chief is Maȟpíya Luta, Scarlet Cloud. The Wasi'chu call him Red Cloud. It was a sacred scarlet sky the morning he was born. We all know he has big medicine, much wisdom..." She trailed off, a note of doubt tinging her words.

"But you ain't sure?" Jessie prodded carefully. "What's he say about the ranchers accusin' his people of stealin' cows from 'em?"

For a few moments, Tasha merely looked into Jessie's eyes. Her expression was almost unreadable, but one thing Jessie was sure of, it wasn't antagonistic. It felt more as if Tasha was searching Jessie's mind for the words she wanted to say. A peculiar feeling, but very real. At last, the proud and graceful Lakota woman spoke again.

"Maȟpíya Luta is a wise man, and honest. The word he says is the thing he does. He believes all men to be so until they show themselves different. I worry it will be too late for our people when the Wasi'chu show themselves to be different."

Jessie couldn't think of a more diplomatic way to say what she knew Tasha was saying. She'd seen it herself. A man's word was cheap, even to himself, in the dog-eat-dog world she had found herself in during the years after leaving her surrogate family and forging her own path in life.

The quiet worry in Tasha's eyes seemed to echo the skittish thoughts of Jessie's own heart. "We got t' trust that there are good Wasi'chu, too," she said, trying as much to comfort herself as Tasha. "Fellas like my brother and Tanner."

"And like my Mato Istime," Tasha said, a dreaminess coming into her voice. Her eyes flitted to the cabin walls, as if she could see through them, all the way to wherever it was Frenchie was fishing or hunting or target shooting with his son.

An unexpected pang of envy shot through Jessie's heart. It almost made her gasp at the suddenness of it. She thrust it aside as quickly as it came, but the thought that came with it would not be so easily silenced. *Must be real fine t' have a man you can worship like Tasha worships Frenchie.*

Abruptly, Tasha focused on Jessie's face once more. "Mato Istime does not trust his own people," she said, her tone tight, her eyes earnest. "My father respects him greatly, and he agrees with him. We are afraid the Wasi'chu are leading Maȟpíya Luta by his nose, like the oxen they use to pull their wagons."

A heavy silence followed. Jessie didn't know what to say.

"I burden you with things too heavy for you." Tasha broke the silence with a soft voice and repentant eyes.

"No. No, you ain't," Jessie protested, shaking her head. "I seen these things myself. I just didn't figure you'd say it so blunt-like is all."

Tanner was just as surprised as she was about Tasha's forthrightness when she shared it with him later that day. They were riding out to check on the herd. "She said that?" he asked incredulously.

"Yup. Straight out, to a Wasi'chu. Just like that."

Tanner shook his head. "Now that beats all," he said, his voice contemplative. "I ain't never heard an Indian speak against his chief."

"Well, she didn't rightly speak against him," Jessie reasoned, as much for her own sake as for Tanner's. "Just figured he ain't walkin' around with his eyes open. I reckon everyone's entitled to their opinion."

"Yeah." Tanner's agreement wasn't backed up by his eyes or his voice.

"What do you figure we're goin' t' do if there's another rustling?" Jessie asked, bringing the conversation back to the task at hand.

There had been no more thefts since the last one, but the longer the days stretched out, the more likely a second strike became. Nobody needed to mention that to anyone else. It weighed on them all like a heavy blanket in summer. All, except Rafe. He seemed impervious to everything going on around him.

Tanner contemplated Jessie's question for a while before replying. "What we're doin' right now. Keep our eyes peeled an' ride every dang inch of this valley till we see something that'll take us in the right direction."

It seemed like the most logical proposition. It wasn't what Jessie had in mind. She wanted to do something more proactive. What, she wasn't entirely sure. Perhaps something that would lure the thieves out into the open, where they'd be exposed. Then they'd know for sure whether Frenchie's suspicions were right. She wished she had some more concrete idea she could expand on.

"Where's the trails that go through here?" Tanner asked out of the blue. "Them Indian trails Frenchie's told us about. You have any idea?"

Jessie shook her head. "Only that they use Crazy Woman Canyon as a pass up into the Bighorn over yonder." She jerked her head to the northwest.

"What say we mosey on over there and see if we can find anything?"

It took them little more than an hour to ride over to the canyon in question. As soon as they came close, Jessie felt a sense of awe stealing over her faculties. The place was magnificent.

Why anyone had given it such an odd name was beyond her. She gazed in deep appreciation at the high vaulting rock walls, the splashing, tumbling creek, and the pungent, patient lodgepole pines standing shoulder to shoulder with clumps of aspen, their roots entwined around boulders streaked with black desert paint.

There was something in the air, something intangible and yet so real it seemed to overpower even the constant muted rumble and roar of rushing water. It wasn't the birdsong or the wildflowers. There was a wildness that refused to be tamed and yet was as gentle as Tasha's kiss against her baby's cheek.

Jessie wished she could stay there forever, soaking in that tender wilderness, feeling her spirit soar above the treetops and over the pointed and angular, unforgiving yet protective boulders.

"Take a looky here," Tanner broke in on Jessie's reverie. "I'd say a couple beeves went this way not too long ago."

Jessie dragged herself back to the present moment and nudged Horace over to where Tanner leaned over his horse's withers, peering at the ground below. Jessie followed his gaze and looked at a mess of cloven hoof prints.

At once, she snapped to attention.

Glancing around, she hoped nobody was watching them. Then she slipped down from the saddle and began leading the horse along what appeared to be a newly created trail. It was difficult to follow. All that really gave it away was trampled underbrush and snapped twigs and branches. Here and there a thick, bovine hair from a mane or perhaps a swishing tail was caught in the fork of a branch or on the rough bark.

Clear hoof prints were few, and all of them were cloven. Jessie had almost despaired of finding anything helpful when the trail opened out onto a sandy beach beside the creek.

Apparently thinking they would not be followed this far, or just not caring at all, the thieves hadn't bothered to cover the tracks. Jessie trotted closer, Horace ambling along behind her.

She peered down at the churned up gravel. Yes. There, crossing the muddle of cows' hoof prints, were tracks made by horses' hooves, all right. Shod horses.

"We got company," Tanner's voice reached her ears just as she straightened up to tell him what she'd found.

A group of horsemen were approaching the other side of the creek. They rode bareback at a spanking pace, making Jessie wonder how she hadn't heard them. As they reached the creek, Jessie realized they were looking right at her and Tanner.

The leader shouted to his companions, and they all halted at the water's edge. Their horses' unshod hooves skidded on the loose gravel beneath as they fought the restraint of the ropes tied around their lower jaws.

The oldest man in the group urged his horse forward into the water of the creek and splashed across without a moment's hesitation. He was saying something in his native language that Jessie couldn't understand.

Dropping Horace's reins, she signed. *We seek peace.*

The leader pulled up his horse barely a foot away from Jessie and glared down at her. He said something over his shoulder to his companions, who were following along behind at a slightly less rabid pace. They laughed.

Jessie thrust out her chin. *Who are you?* she signed. *Why are you here?* Jessie heard the creak of buffalo sinew and the scrape of wood against wood.

She instantly knew one man was nocking an arrow to his bow. She dared not look at him, instead holding the gaze of the man in front of her.

His eyes narrowed as he raised his hand. The buffalo sinew creaked again. Jessie silently let out her breath and studied the man before her. His eyes were heavy lidded above an imposing hawk nose, a wide, stern mouth, and a folded chin. His face was long and square and stony, like the great boulders all around them. His black eyes seemed all-observing, cutting through her, down to her soul.

Still she held her shoulders back and her chin lifted.

You do not ask me this. I ask you, the man signed in reply to her questions.

We work for Mato Istime, Jessie responded, hoping they were Sioux. *We seek cattle that are lost.* Under the circumstances, she thought it wiser not to say stolen.

The man's face relaxed slightly, but his eyes lost none of their alertness, or perhaps a better word would have been wariness. Without taking those eyes from Jessie's face, he motioned one of his companions closer, giving what sounded like a clipped command.

The man came forward, reining in his horse beside the older man's. "This is Chief Red Cloud of the Oglala Lakota," the man said in halting English.

Chapter 6
Refutable Proof

Behind Jessie, Tanner burst into a paroxysm of coughing while Jessie simply stared at Red Cloud uncomprehendingly. She had heard and understood what the other man had said, but her brain refused to accept it.

The corner of Red Cloud's mouth twitched, as if he were trying not to laugh. Jessie herself felt close to laughing out loud, but the knowledge that she stood before a feared warrior helped keep her in check.

The crow has pecked out your tongue? Red Cloud signed.

"Ah, no," Jessie stammered, recovering her wits. Then she paused and looked at the younger man. "I can speak English?" she asked.

Instead of translating her question into Lakota, the interpreter simply looked at his leader in silence.

Red Cloud, whose face had once again turned to stark granite, nodded slowly and said, "Ha," in a flat tone.

"He say yes."

"I figured," Jessie muttered, certain they did not hear her.

Red Cloud was speaking again.

"He say you must speak truth. We see men who take all the meat for themselves, riding along our sacred trails. You are with them?" the man translated rapidly.

"If they had a bunch of cows with 'em, they're the fellas we're lookin' for, but they ain't with us. They're against us," Tanner butted in.

No cows. Wagons before, but no wagons this time. Red Cloud signed, and Jessie repeated his words out loud for Tanner's benefit.

"Men with wagons?" Jessie asked. "You mean settlers?"

The younger man looked at his leader, seeming to ask permission to speak freely. The great war chief nodded, and the young man continued. "Many wagons, women, children, horses, men. They try to cross our land. Say they go make new home where the yellow iron is in the rivers. Red Cloud say no. Sitting Bull say no. Spotted Tail say no. Even He-Rides-a-White-Man's-Horse say no."

Red Cloud snorted derisively at the mention of the last chief's name. Jessie detected a flash of antagonism and disdain in his eyes.

"So the wagons turn back," the young man went on. "But now we go to powwow with Chief Black Kettle and Chief Dull Knife, our Cheyenne brothers. On the way, we see nine white men on our land. One of them is the man called Bozeman. He who had the wagons, he who offered money for our sacred lands." He spat on the ground beside his horse, his face and eyes full of contempt.

Jessie looked at Tanner, her eyes wide and questioning. What could they possibly say to these men? Red Bull signed again, negating any need for her to speak.

The white man, he who takes all the meat for himself, he has stripped the land of buffalo, of deer, of elk, even of rabbits. There is nothing left. Nothing left for my people to live the way we must, the ancient ways. Now we have this valley. We will not let he who takes all the meat for himself take this valley too.

"What's he sayin'?" Tanner hissed in a loud whisper.

Jessie had no chance to reply. The young man was speaking again, his voice rising and falling with the same emphasis and passion his chief's signs had held.

"We cannot drive them away. If we chase them, they will fight. If they fight, we will fight. That will give he who takes all the meat for himself an excuse to make war and take our valley, just like he took the grasslands in the south from our brothers there. We will not give him an excuse. We will not harm him. But we do not trust this Bozeman."

Well, Red Cloud was indeed wary of the white man and his promises of peace and autonomy. Jessie held the war chief's gaze for a moment longer.

Behind the glittering, stone cold eyes, she thought she detected a shimmer of appreciation and respect. She wondered how many could look him in the eye. Then, suddenly, she wondered how she found it so easy. Perhaps because she had nothing to hide.

You will find your cows over the next rise, then to the right. Follow the little creek until the great tree at the mouth of the small canyon. They are there with the white man who stole them, Red Cloud signed gravely.

Jessie raised her eyebrows and then quickly pulled her face straight. It might not be a good idea to look surprised. He might think she didn't believe him or suspected that he had taken them to begin with.

"Thank you, Chief," she said in the most respectful voice she could muster, but Red Cloud was already turning away, his horse splashing across the Crazy Woman Creek to join the men who had stayed on the other side. They were putting away their bows and arrows, and Jessie only then realized she and Tanner had had cold, razor-sharp steel aimed at them the whole time.

Before she could fully gather her wits and comprehend what had just happened, Red Cloud and his men were gone. Only the distant sound of their horses' hooves echoing off the walls of the canyon was proof they had been there at all.

"What'd he say at the end there?" Tanner broke in on her thoughts.

"He told me where t' find our cows," she said, the words sounding surreal in her mouth.

Red Cloud's directions led them straight to a smaller, elevated canyon leading cut from the greater one. A huddle of about fifteen yearling cows and bulls stood grazing in the center where a patch of thatch grass grew.

Under an overhang at the end of the canyon was a lone cowhand. His horse browsed on some sagebrush. As soon as they entered the canyon, he sprang to his feet, reaching immediately for his gun.

It was a fairly useless action. The distance between them was too great for him to make an accurate shot. Jessie scanned the hides of the yearlings. They had Frenchie's initials branded on them, all right. The E halfway over the B and the F stuck onto the end of the E. A body couldn't miss it.

"Howdy, stranger!" Tanner called out.

Jessie shot him a curious glance. He winked at her, and she instantly knew she'd better play his game.

"Who's there?" came the careful reply in much less carefree tones.

"Name's Tanner Nugent. Just signed on at the BEF Ranch. You know it?" Tanner dismounted and sauntered closer.

Jessie felt her throat tighten. If that cowboy had really taken these cows, he might get jittery enough to shoot. She couldn't understand what Tanner was up to. She hoped he did.

"Sure. Sure, I do." The cowhand was still gripping his revolver, though the barrel was thankfully pointing to the ground.

"We saw some Indians a way back, figured they took our cows an' holed 'em up here somewhere," Tanner went on. A light flickered in Jessie's mind as Tanner went on. "You see 'em? Or did you just get here?"

"Indians?" the cowhand stammered. Then, his voice taking on a much bolder tone, he exclaimed, "Oh, yeah! I saw 'em drivin' this packet an' figured they must've stole 'em from some poor sod."

"Well, that poor sod happens t' be our boss," Jessie added, warming to Tanner's strategy.

"Frenchie? These are Frenchie's cows?" the cowhand quavered, returning his pistol to its holster and stepping closer.

"They sure are. See the brand?" Tanner gestured to the nearest yearling.

By now, the cowhand had reached them. He made a great show of peering at the hairless lines on the animal's rump. "The hell you say," he muttered.

"Who you ride for?" Jessie asked.

Tanner shot her a cautioning look, but it was too late. The cowhand looked immediately flustered.

"I, ah, don't ride for a brand. Bit of a saddle tramp," he said. "After I chased off them Indians, I figured I'd just have me a nap before I go find the owner."

Afterward, when Jessie told the story around the supper table, Frenchie frowned so deeply that his eyebrows met in the middle. "Tell me again what he looked like," he insisted.

Jessie did, but Frenchie couldn't seem to connect her description to any of the regular cowhands he knew about these parts.

"Must be a greenhorn, fresh hired, or else he really is a saddle tramp," he muttered. Then he looked up and held Tanner's gaze. "Y'all know what this means, don't ya?"

"It ain't Lakota stealin' our cows," Tanner said darkly.

"Reckon I better warn the others," Frenchie said. "First thing tomorrow," he added. "Then we better take the bunch of yearlings down t' Laramie. Best sell as many as we can before they're all rustled."

***

Fort Laramie was bustl ng with life when they arrived a week later. A large wagon train was passing through. Staying for a few days, in fact, as Waters informed Frenchie when he and the others collected the money for the cattle.

"I'd say you brought this lot in at exactly the right time," Waters said expansively, taking a long draw on a cigar he was enjoying along with his habitual afternoon bourbon. "They'll sell like hotcakes, no doubt about it." He regarded Frenchie for a moment through the drifting, curling smoke. "I must admit, though, I'm curious why you're so eager to be rid of your stock, Frenchie. The situation getting that bad, is it?"

The corners of Frenchie's mouth pulled his mustache deeper into his beard. "I was fixin' t' have a parley with some of the other fellers if they're hereabouts," he growled. "Got some questions for 'em."

Waters showed no emotion. "You'll find them over at Old Bedlam." He took another pull on the cigar and stared past them.

"Thank you, sir," Frenchie said, tapping the brim of his hat with two fingers. He turned on his heel, marching between Jessie and Danny toward Old Bedlam.

Jessie caught Tanner's eye with a here-comes-trouble look before they both started out after their new boss.

Even if Waters hadn't told them where to find the other ranchers, they would have been drawn by the loud babble coming from the soldiers' barracks. If it could be called a barracks. The room they'd last seen the drama society rehearsing in was now filled with soldiers and ranchers, hotly decrying something.

At first it was just a babble of words, but then the hubbub subsided slightly as a strident voice cut through the rest like a whip crack.

"They ain't gonna lick us, fellers. You mind my words. We'll whip 'em good an' teach them long-fingered savages a thing or two."

Jessie stopped and stared at the man who had spoken. It was none other than Gale Bates, the man who had told her she wouldn't see him coming before she'd eaten his bullet. At the moment the thought crossed her mind, he looked up and saw her. His eyes narrowed for a split second, and Jessie knew he'd recognized her.

For a moment longer, he glared at her, devilment in his eyes. Then his gaze moved on, and a self-satisfied smirk played across his features. "Ain't that so, Frenchie?" he asked in the same grating, insistent tone.

"Oh, there's some long-fingered savages stealin' from us all right," Frenchie replied dryly, planting his feet in a belligerent stance and crossing his arms over his broad chest. "What I'm wonderin' is, are they red-skinned or white-skinned savages?"

A collective gasp rose from the gathered men, all eyes turning to see who had spoken.

"Always shovin' a stick in the spokes, ain't ya, Frenchie?" another voice asked rhetorically.

Jessie identified the speaker as the Mr. Crawford she and her comrades had almost gone to work for. His eyes were as hard and haughty as Gale Bates's.

"If your meanin' is that I'm always askin' questions that needs askin', then yeah, I reckon I am." Either Frenchie hadn't picked up that Crawford's question didn't require an answer, or he was deliberately giving him the one he knew Crawford didn't want to hear.

Bates stood to his feet, nearly upsetting the small table that stood beside his chair, holding his drink and a box of cigars. "You!" he spat venomously, his nostrils flared and his eyes flashing with the fire of hades.

"You're a disgrace to your own race is what you are. No loyalty to your own kind. Why don't ya cut dirt back to your squaw and your half-breeds an' leave it t' real men t' get shut of those thievin' varmints?"

Jessie sucked in her breath, her hands ready over her LeMats. Out of the corner of her eye, she saw Tanner's fingers moving closer to his holster. Danny gave a little moan of fearful anticipation.

But it soon became clear, if there was going to be a shoot up, it wouldn't be Frenchie who started it. The silence hung so thick, Jessie felt like she could grab a handful of it if she had a mind to.

Instead, she cut it with a question of her own. "Say, Mr. Bates," she said in a deliberately conversational tone, "you know any Indians in the habit of shoein' their horses?"

Bates shifted his glare from Frenchie to her, a flicker of distraction crossing his face. "What're ya drivin' at?" he growled.

"Well, we found us some of Frenchie's cattle that were run off, an' they were driven by fellas ridin' shoed horses. Read it plain as daylight in the tracks," Tanner explained. "We got t' wonderin' which tribe likes t' shoe their horses an' where they hide their blacksmiths."

Jessie had to swallow down a smile. She and Tanner were becoming pretty good at reading each other's minds. It made her feel kind of warm and fuzzy inside. She forced her attention back to the situation unfolding in front of her. A buzz of murmuring had sprung up like a mountain wind bringing a blizzard.

"Ha!" Bates laughed humorlessly. "You stupid enough t' think an Indian won't steal a shod horse so he can rustle beeves?"

"Well, no," Jessie shot back. "But my brother and one of the other hands saw…" Her words faded in her mouth as she felt fingers digging into her arm. She turned her head to look into Danny's worried eyes.

No, he mouthed silently, turning his head ever so slightly from side to side. Jessie inhaled slowly. What did Danny know that she didn't?

"I don't give a continental what you an' your posse *think* y'all saw," Bates snarled, relieving Jessie of the need to cover up her close blunder. "It's plain as the enormous nose on Frenchie's face that Indians are takin' our cattle an' bein' consarned bold about it, too."

A roar of agreement erupted all around him, laced with threats of retaliation and revenge.

Frenchie stared at them for a while and then shook his head. "Don't say I didn't warn ya, fellers," he said, only loud enough for those closest to him to hear. Then he turned on his heel and walked away.

Jessie, Tanner, and Danny followed suit.

"Yeah, that's right, get your sorry carcass back to your squaw, Frenchie. You an' your Indian-lovin' buddies!" Bates yelled after them.

As they reached their horses and Jessie stepped her left foot into the stirrup, Danny gripped her arm again. "I couldn't tell ya in front of all of them," he said, jerking his head back toward Old Bedlam.

"Tell us what, Danny?" Jessie asked, alarm shooting through her heart at the look in her brother's eyes.

"That Bates fella, he was there, too."

Jessie's blood froze in her veins. She knew what Danny was going to say next before he had finished drawing breath.

"He was out there on Frenchie's ranch with Rafe and the Wilson fella the night I saw 'em."

Chapter 7
Treaty

As soon as they reached home a couple of days later, Jessie went to Tasha.

"We got t' get to your Chief Maȟpíya Lúta," she said earnestly. "You got t' help me find him."

Tasha looked up from picking pine nuts out of the cones. Her gaze was curious, although none of the usual calmness had left her eyes. "You wish an audience with Oglala Chief?" Her tone sounded almost amused.

Jessie swallowed down the rising irritation in her chest. Tasha's composure was enviable, alluring. It was also a trifle frustrating sometimes.

"There's danger," she said, hoping Tasha would latch on to the seriousness of the situation. "There's a fella name of Gale Bates. He's sayin' your people are the ones stealin' the cows. He's gettin' everybody riled up an' angry."

"Ah, yes. Gale Bates," Tasha said reflectively. "I call him Tatekata. He is just like the hot winds that come from the mountains but bring no rain."

Jessie fleetingly wondered how Gale Bates might react to being called that to his face, but immediately dragged her thoughts back to her request. "Can you take me to him? To

Maȟpíya Lúta? He's got t' know what's happening, and I got t' make sure he hears it all."

"I will take you," Tasha said. "But I cannot make him listen to you."

"Fair enough," Jessie agreed. Even if she had to sit outside the war chief's home for an entire week before he granted her an audience, so be it. But she had to see him.

The two women, with Frenchie's permission, set out the next day. Jessie politely turned down Tanner's offer to accompany them for protection.

"I can handle myself," she said. "I'm thinkin' Red Cloud'll be more likely t' listen to me if I come alone with Tasha."

"It ain't Red Cloud I'm frettin' over," Tanner said, avoiding Jessie's eyes.

"Who then? Rafe? Bates?"

The look on Tanner's face told her she was right. "Why don't you an' Danny ride along behind us a ways? Keep an eye out like that?"

Frenchie agreed to the idea, and they hit the trail. Tasha wasn't sure where exactly her people would be camped, although she had an idea of the general location. After a couple hours of searching, they came upon the village. While they were still far off, they were spotted and their approach loudly and excitedly announced.

Children rushed out to meet them, followed by a pack of barking, bounding dogs, as they slipped down from their horses and walked the rest of the way. Tipi flaps were flung open and cooking fires abandoned as the people of Tasha's village came out en masse to see what the commotion was about.

As the children reached them, they began chanting Tasha's name over and over, dancing around the two women as if they were a conquering army returned from taming far-flung lands. Tasha's smile was serene, filled with happy contentment. She had clearly come home. Once again, Jessie felt a brief pang of jealousy.

Tasha, as if sensing the turmoil in her companion's spirit, placed a gentle hand on Jessie's shoulder as they entered the village. She kept it there while she greeted everyone, babbling away in her mother tongue. The children peppered her with what sounded like questions, if the tone of their voices was anything to go by. Tasha responded with rapid, kindly sounding words.

At last, the hubbub died down and the people parted like prairie grass when the wind blows through it. Before them, a pathway opened up, flanked by happy but curious faces. Hands reached out tentatively to touch Jessie on her shoulder and her arm as she passed, Tasha's hand still firmly on her other shoulder. At last, they stood before a large tipi with neatly stitched hides covering it.

It was painted all over with scenes of hunting and war, of the sun and animals and mountains, of people and fires and symbols Jessie couldn't decipher. The scent of wood smoke and burned sage reached her nostrils, along with the earthy aroma of leather and animal fur.

"Maȟpíya Lúta waits for us," Tasha said softly. "He heard of our coming and wishes to speak with you, Strong Woman."

Jessie hesitated for a breathless moment. "He calls me that?"

Tasha's eyes twinkled. "Maȟpíya Lúta sees more than his eyes can show him."

Jessie swallowed, though her throat was dry, and followed Tasha into the tipi, ducking her head into the entrance. In the center was the firepit, as she had expected, and beyond it sat Maȟpíya Lúta, his stony features softened in the interior's haziness.

He held a peace pipe in his hands. White smoke drifted from the bowl, caught in the single ray of light shining through a partially opened flap in the tipi's top. Tasha sat down on the sand just beyond the entrance, gently pulling Jessie down beside her.

Tasha said something in Lakota, and Maȟpíya Lúta responded in his deep, guttural voice. Then he looked at Jessie. *You wish to tell me something,* he signed.

"Yeah, something important," Jessie confirmed his statement.

I am listening.

"Gale Bates, the rancher, is stirrin' up trouble," she stated simply. "There's been some real big cattle thefts, an' he's sayin' it's your people. I figure he's lumpin' the Cheyenne an' the Arapahoe into this, too, seein' as he don't know the difference."

He can say what he likes. That does not make it true.

Jessie hesitated. "Yeah, I know that. Trouble is Bates don't know it. In his head, y'all are guilty, an' he's rilin' up everybody around him t', well, t' take matters into their own hands."

You believe they will attack us? Try to take back the cattle he says we stole?

"That's about the long an' the short, Chief." Jessie realized she was clasping and unclasping her hands. The look on Maȟpíya Lúta's face did not speak of a man who felt worry or concern, despite what she was saying to him as clearly as she could without sounding alarmist.

Why do you warn us?

The question took Jessie by surprise. "Why? Well, I ain't sure it's any of your people that's stealin' anything, and it ain't right t' punish folks if ya can't prove they're guilty."

You're not sure.

"Yeah. I seen hoof prints that belong to horses with shoes, an' I seen cows missin', but I ain't seen any cows here. And we have caught nobody drivin' 'em off." She hoped her answer was satisfactory.

They will not attack us.

Jesse wondered how he could be so sure. Her answer came as he went on signing.

We have a treaty with the white man's Big White Chief. The treaty protects us.

"Tell that t' Gale Bates," Jessie said darkly.

What is your meaning?

"My meanin' is Gale Bates don't care about your treaty. He'll start trouble any way he can, an' he'll put the blame squarely on you folks. Who d'you think the Big White Chief is goin' t' believe? You or his own people?"

Maȟpíya Lúta regarded her silently for a few moments. Then he leaned to his right and whispered to a man Jessie only now noticed, sitting further back in the shadows. A short, low-voiced discussion ensued. Then Maȟpíya Lúta turned back.

I speak to White Eagle. We thank you for your warning. It is welcome and good. There is nothing to be done now, but if the white man makes war with us, we will get the army to help us.

"The army?" Jessie's eyes widened in disbelief. Surely, he couldn't believe they would help him.

Yes, the army. The treaty says the army must help us if we are attacked by their people. We will speak with Major Wood if there is trouble.

"Truth be told, I was fixin' t' go to him myself," Jessie said. "Me an' my friends, we've seen enough t' give cause for doubt about who stole those cows."

Maȟpíya Lúta held up his hand and the look in his eyes told Jessie she had talked too much.

"If you'd like me to, I'll do it. But only if you'd like me to."

The war chief held her gaze in a long silence.

You have a big heart, Strong Woman, he signed. *May the Great Mystery watch over you as he watches over us.*

Jessie felt suddenly small. She lowered her eyes and stared at her boots. Strong Woman. She wasn't sure she deserved that name. Sometimes she felt like her actions were all rooted in fear, as bold as they might seem to the casual observer. Still, something told her Maȟpíya Lúta was not merely a casual observer.

The Sioux war chief went back to puffing on his pipe again, while White Eagle, still obscured by the shadows in the corner behind his leader, spoke some more in a low voice, Maȟpíya Lúta nodding slowly as he listened.

"We go now," Tasha said, taking Jessie's arm and helping her to her feet.

The next moment, they were outside, blinking in the harsh sunlight. The village had gone back to its activities, except for a few curious individuals. They immediately began showering questions on Tasha again, but she held up her free hand, the other arm still linked with Jessie's, and began leading her white friend away.

"The treaty with the Big White Chief means much to our people," she spoke as they mounted up.

Turning her horse's head back toward her other home, she kept speaking, and Jessie nudged Horace forward, not wanting to miss anything the woman had to say. She noticed that Tasha never spoke unless it was necessary.

"Many of our chiefs and our bravest warriors keep the treaty papers sealed up and safe in clay jars. Maȟpíya Lúta was there with his uncle in the white man's year called 1851, when he was not yet chief. He tells how there were many, many people, from all tribes, north and south, east and west. For days they gathered, so many men, women, and children. They covered the hills like grass.

"Lakota, Shoshone, Crow, Assiniboine, Snake, Cheyenne, Mandan, and many more. Only the fiercest war tribes, the Comanche, the Kiowa, and the Apache, they did not come. Our nations camped with wide spaces between. They said it was for their horses to all have grass, but Maȟpíya Lúta says he knew it was because they would fight."

"Makes sense," Jessie said. "Was there any fightin'?"

"Yes," Tasha replied. "Some Cheyenne warriors killed two Shoshone. There was much loud talking. Maȟpíya Lúta says he feared there would be a great war with so many warriors in one place, and the treaty would not happen. But the leaders of the Cheyenne agreed to cover the bodies of the Shoshone in apology. They made a grand feast for them."

"And the Shoshone accepted?" Jessie asked, so caught up in the story, she let Horace's reins hang loose while he followed Tasha's horse.

"They did. They took the gifts, and there was much talking. I think you white people say speeching." Tasha smiled at Jessie.

"Oh, yeah. Makin' speeches." Jessie returned the smile. "Looks like that's a problem all of us have."

Tasha laughed. "And so there was peace, and the treaty was signed. But the nations waited for many more days on the plains, waiting for the gifts to come and the food the speaker of the Big White Chief had promised. The people did not leave. It had been promised, and that meant it would come. It did come many days later when the people were getting restless. There was talk that the boats bringing it had been cursed with the big cramps and that made the coming slow." She shivered involuntarily.

"Cholera?" Jessie remarked with raised eyebrows. "I've heard your people suffer a sight more than white folks do from that," she said sympathetically. "And it's pretty terrible even for us."

Tasha nodded, her face somber. "Yes. It is a terrible thing. Many die."

A moment of silence passed between them. Then Jessie asked what she had been burning to ask. "Tasha, I got t' know. Do you really believe the Big White Chief will protect your nations if white men try t' settle on your lands or do ya harm?"

Tasha looked at her, reining her horse from a brisk trot to a slow walk. "They have given their word, and in our culture, it is bad medicine to break our word. But I have seen the white men. There are many who speak words and throw them to the wind. They do not keep them even a day. I know there are some among our people who do the same. I can only hope your Big White Chief is not like some people he rules."

Jessie sighed. There it was. Just as she learned. The folks at the top of the hierarchy in any society were all deluding themselves if they thought for a moment they could control every single human being under their jurisdiction. What bothered her more was how many of the officials themselves really, truly took their treaties seriously.

* * *

Hastings took in his surroundings with a sense of pleasant surprise. He'd heard many tales of army forts, even seen a few himself, and they always gave him a sense of deprivation and cowardice. Fort Laramie did not subscribe to either of those descriptions from what he could recall from his previous visit.

He could almost imagine he was at West Point. At least the size of the place, coupled with the lack of a wall, the soldiers' dress, and the sound of a band practicing some waltz of Schubert's echoed through the prestigious school. To say nothing of the presence of womenfolk and children who could only be the wives and families of some of the officers.

"I wouldn't be surprised if they held a ball here once a month," he muttered to himself as he stepped up to the row of offices where the commanding officers spent at least some of their time, he hoped.

The metallic rap of the brass doorknocker elicited a "Who is it?" in a less than enthusiastic tone.

"Major Wood, it's Richard Hastings. We've met before and we've been corresponding."

Hastings was still drawing breath to say more when the door suddenly opened. A young soldier stood there but stepped back so Hastings could see into the room. It smelled of cigar smoke, dust, and peppermints.

"Please come in, Mr. Hastings, the major said. "It's good to see you again. How may I assist you?"

"Thank you, kindly, Major," Hastings replied, stepping past the soldier. "You remember the content of our letters, I presume?"

"Of course. Take a seat." Major Wood indicated a chair in front of his desk. The soldier disappeared, closing the door behind him. "As I informed you in my letters, there are already ample ranchers supplying the emigrants with oxen. Building anything other than forts within the boundaries of the areas demarcated for the local tribes is expressly forbidden according to the terms of the treaty."

"Ah, yes, I remember you mentioned that. However, I thought I'd like to come have a closer look for myself." Hastings settled himself into the brocade-upholstered, carved mahogany chair offered him.

"No law against that," Wood offered, folding his hands in front of him, his elbows on the desk. "I must warn you, though. There's little anybody can do about that treaty and what it means. Of course, if you'd like to cash in on the western expansion, I'm sure there's more than enough opportunity to go around along the Emigrant Road."

"The Emigrant Road is mostly staked out already," Hastings replied. "I'd like to be part of something new before it becomes overrun."

"Which makes perfect sense," Major Wood agreed. "Trouble is, there isn't as much space to go around here as there is along the Emigrant Road."

Hastings didn't need telling that he and the major were talking at cross purposes. Nothing the major said could dissuade him from getting what he wanted, and nothing he said would budge the major to give him some kind of direction to work in. That much was clear to him. "Well I suppose there's nothing left to do but for me to amuse myself exploring the area and getting to know some locals. There's no treaty against that, is there, Major?" He offered the man a benign smile to sugarcoat his words.

The major didn't crack a smile. "Not one that I know of, Mr. Hastings. Now, if you'll excuse me, I have rather a lot of work to do."

"Of course. Thank you again for your valuable time, Major Wood." Hastings rose from his seat, inclined his head, and left the major's office. He hadn't expected to make much headway. The next order of business was to see who else he was dealing with.

The sound of laughter drifted across from the bachelor officers' quarters. What had they called it again? Ah, yes, Old Bedlam. Rather appropriate. He sauntered across and inserted himself in the company of men sitting around and playing cards, reading books, or joining in the lively conversation that was happening among some less studious individuals.

One man caught his eye. He was definitely not a soldier. His dress was that of a cowhand, a range rider. Just the man Hastings was looking for. Sidling over, Hastings introduced himself and asked if he could share the sofa the man sat on.

"Oh, sure, mister. It's big enough." A hazy smile from equally hazy eyes told Hastings his new friend was well lubricated. Even better. "Where you from, mister?"

"Me? Why, I'm just a clueless city fellow from Boston. But you look like a man who was born and raised in the saddle."

The compliment worked. "Aw, shucks, naw. I'm just a regular cowpoke, nothin' special," the man drawled. "But if you were lookin' t' try your luck at ridin' and ropin', well, I'm your man."

"Really?" Hastings replied with mock surprise. "How fortuitous."

"I reckon it is. Anything you want to know about ranchin', I'll tell ya. Naw, I'll show ya, mister."

"Well, splendid! I was hoping I could have a look at all the ranches around here. I'm fascinated by ranching, you know? Would you be able to introduce me to all the ranchers? Let me know how much stock is on their land? How about the Indians? Are they much trouble?"

The man grinned past his day-old stubble. "Just so happens, I've taken a few days' leave. How about I show ya around? I'll answer all your questions and then some, mister."

"You have got yourself a deal, young fellow."

Chapter 8
Vigil

"Tanner, why d'you suppose Red Cloud would have told us where that passel of beeves was the other day?" Jessie asked thoughtfully while the two of them watched over Frenchie's main flock, grazing in a grass-laden valley near Crazy Woman Canyon.

Tanner narrowed his eyes. "Why don't you just tell me what you're anglin' at?" he replied with a wink.

"Humor me," Jessie shot back, wishing he wouldn't wink at her. It made her feel like a girl instead of the cowhand she was.

"Well, let's see now, if I don't figure in what I know about Frenchie an' his dealings with Red Cloud's lot, I reckon there's two reasons a fella would do that. First off, the cowpoke sleepin' beside 'em was right, an' Red Cloud wanted to lead us down the garden path, or second off, Red Cloud straight up wanted t' help us and he and his men really are innocent."

Jessie nodded, not taking her eyes from the hillsides around the brown backs with their swishing tails and slowly bobbing heads scattered about the valley. "That's what I figured, too. An' I got to askin' myself, why did that cowpoke look so ready to shoot when we first came in there?"

"Maybe he was still spooked from fighting off Indians." Tanner shrugged.

"That's another thing that don't sit right with me. Tanner, that fella would've been missing a heap of hair if he'd tried t' fight off Red Cloud and his men. Hardly likely he'd be sucking air at all, let alone shuckin' his firin' iron and jumpin' up to see who's comin'."

"You mean, if it looks like a skunk, an' it stinks like a skunk, chances are it's a skunk. Is that about right?" Tanner sounded a little amused.

"That's exactly right," Jessie agreed. "An' things sure do stink. Yesterday, when I spoke with Red Cloud, I felt pretty darn sure they weren't the ones rustlin' those beeves. Now folks could say I'm just bein' taken in by the fella, but chew on this: why would he be stealin' cows from his own kin? If everybody but Frenchie's cows was disappearin', I'd say Bates is onto somethin'. But Frenchie's sufferin' just as hard as the rest of 'em, if not worse."

"Howdy, pardners!" Danny's voice cut in on Jessie's reasonings. "I brought y'all some grub. Tasha wanted to make sure y'all weren't starvin' out here."

"Thanks, Dan," Tanner said, gratefully taking a parcel from Danny's outstretched hand.

"Sure thing," Danny replied. "Anythin' happenin' here?"

"Naw, not so you'd notice," Jessie replied before she ripped off a piece of pemmican and chewed. She closed her eyes appreciatively.

"Jessie's figurin' who's stealin' the cows," Tanner informed Danny.

"You figured it out already?" Danny spoke past a cheek full of pemmican as he stared at his sister, wide eyed.

"I've figured it ain't Red Cloud and his lot." Jessie swallowed and ripped off another piece. There just wasn't anything like real pemmican made by someone who knew how the process passed down from generations of Lakota.

"Yeah, I figured that too. Seems too easy to just blame the Indians. I've seen me a lot of that around." Danny gazed out at the cattle, and the sound of cicadas rose to fill the silence between them.

"Don't you fellas want to figure out who is doin' this?" Jessie asked, feeling at once agitated.

"Well, sure," Danny said. "Question is how?"

"We can start by askin' the questions nobody else is askin'. Like why would Red Cloud steal his own kin's cows?"

"They'd say it was the Cheyenne or the Arapahoe," Danny said.

"Okay how about the tracks we found, all shoed horses?"

"You heard Bates's argument against that yourself," Tanner reminded her.

"Well, somebody's got t' do something!" Jessie fumed. "Bates an' his posse are blowin' up t' start a war, here, an' all he's got is lies. Those Lakota ain't guilty, an' I'll be danged if I'll stand by while they're murdered and their villages torched for the sake of a few cows."

"We'd best keep our noses out of it," Tanner cautioned. "We're here t' watch Frenchie's cattle and keep 'em safe from wolves…"

"An' rustlers," Jessie added in unison with him at the end. "So why ain't we goin' after the varmint who stole those forty head?"

"Because we don't know who did it, an' we ain't the army or the rangers," Tanner countered.

"Well, I'm sure as hell goin' to do everythin' I know how t' find out who did it. You can bet your bottom dollar on that!" Jessie huffed. Horace fidgeted beneath the saddle, shifting his weight and tossing his head as if he felt Jessie's ire and agreed with it.

"Jessie, just leave it be, will ya, please?" Danny pleaded, giving Tanner a worried glance. "Your life ain't worth a few head of cows."

"What are you two not telling me?" Jessie said warily.

"Nothin', sis. Your guess is as good as ours about what's shakin' out on this ranch. All we're askin' is that you let the folks handle it who's supposed to handle it."

"We don't want t' see you hurt, Jessie," Tanner said gruffly, gazing out over the herd.

"So that's it? You two reckon I can't take care of myself?"

They didn't reply. Tanner shook his head and looked away so she couldn't see his face. Danny looked at her pleadingly.

Jessie shook her head. "All those years I handled myself real well out there in New Mexico Territory, I'll have y'all know. Didn't need a babysitter, that's for sure! Didn't need nobody tellin' me where I should keep my nose out t' save my hide, neither. You fellas can do what ya darn well want, but I aim t' do my job the best way I know how, an' ain't nobody goin' t' stop me, so don't the two of you even try!"

Her temper was out of control. She wanted to spin Horace right around and ride clear over to the other side of the herd, where she'd be away from the two condescending men she'd thought were on her side all this time. Instead, she sat and seethed. With rustlers around, probably alerted to the fact she was looking out for ones with white skins, too, it wasn't safe.

For a long while, a tense silence hung between them. Jessie tried to distract herself by inspecting every little dip and gully in the valley below. She tried to imagine where rustlers would hide and by what route they'd drive the cattle in order to keep tracks to a minimum, as well as be less conspicuous, less visible. They'd for sure want some kind of cover, and there was plenty of that, but they'd still have to go over some exposed areas, out in the bright sunshine. It would be better if...

She stopped mid-thought, an idea taking shape in her mind. She couldn't dare tell Tanner or Danny about it. No, she'd keep it quiet, but it just might be the ticket.

If it proved her suspicions correct, she could just call in the others. Working alone was better with figuring things out. White people made too much noise. They hadn't learned to move quietly, like the Apache and the Sioux.

"Jessie, you know I care about ya, don't ya?" Danny interrupted her thoughts.

"Sure, I do," Jessie muttered, feeling slightly guilty about her flare up now that she'd calmed down a little and there was a glimmer of hope on the horizon that there was actually something she could do about the rustlers.

"I don't mean t' talk down to ya. Truth is, me and Tanner both know you're more than fit t' take care of yourself. It's just, well, I guess I still feel bad for lettin' ya run away from the Mansfields all by yourself."

Jessie's head snapped round to look at her brother. "Now you're discombobulatin' me," she said. "We both decided it was for the best, an' we both agreed. It's just the way it was, Danny. You know that. Don't ya?"

"It is, and it ain't." Danny shrugged, looking haunted. "We were just kids who'd grown up in a fort and on a ranch. What did we know about the real world? The one full of dangers we'd never heard of an' folks who looked all right but who'd bamboozle ya soon as look at ya. Or shoot ya on a notion."

Jessie stared at him, seeing with new eyes the boy she had grown up with, now a man and himself looking at life through different eyes.

"I never told you nor anyone else, but since I watched you disappear in the darkness that night, never one day went by that I didn't wish I'd gone with ya. Especially when I got older an' I saw what men out in the world are like and how hard it is for a woman..." Danny faltered. "I mean..."

"It's all right, Danny. I hear ya," Jessie reassured him. "Don't pay me no mind. I'm just a little tense, is all."

"I reckon we all are," Tanner said quietly.

His words echoed through Jessie's mind that night when she snuck out of the bunkhouse and fetched Horace from the corral. Saddling up, she led him from the homestead and headed out to the meadows and hillsides shrouded in darkness. Only darkness would give the rustlers the cover they needed.

If they were planning to steal more of Frenchie's cows, by thunder she'd find them, if it meant she had to survive on but a few hours of sleep a night for the next couple of weeks.

As she rode along, listening and watching for the sounds of cattle and horsemen, she looked up at the stars, marveling that even in the darkest of nights, there always seemed to be some kind of light to illuminate the Earth. It was as if darkness could never really fully take over from light. As if darkness itself needed light to be seen and to see.

Her thoughts kept her awake on that first night, and the second and the third. Thoughts of Bates and Red Cloud and Frenchie. Thoughts of the wagon trains that wanted to ride through the agreed-upon territory of the people who had been there first, the people who had learned how to live off the land changing nothing about it.

To her mind, it took some kind of skill to move about, living in different areas, and leave hardly a sign that there had ever been a village erected there. White folks couldn't manage that. They seemed intent on leaving some kind of mark to show they had been somewhere. Most of the time, it ended up being nothing but an ugly scar. Not only on the land, but on other people's souls, too.

While her thoughts were fruitful, her nightly vigils delivered no rustlers. Still, she couldn't give up. They would have to strike again some time or another, and she was determined to be there when they did.

***

Frenchie unsaddled his horse and let her out into the large corral behind the house. He headed for the kitchen, his brow furrowed in thought. Jessie had looked pretty darn tuckered out that morning when he'd gone out with them to ride the range and check on the animals.

There seemed to be none missing, and he'd left them to brand a few calves who were ready. He wanted to spend some time mending the couple of leaks in the cabin roof and chopping wood for the woodpile.

As he reached the door, Tasha opened it. Her face was serene and unruffled as always, but her eyes told a different story. "Bates is at the front," she whispered. "With some other men." There was no need for her to say any more.

"Bolt the door and take the little ones down to our basement," Frenchie whispered. "I'll go round the side of the house."

Tasha inclined her head, a steely determination coming into her eyes, and closed the door again. Frenchie skirted the cabin and first peered past the corner of the porch so he could gauge the mood of his visitors.

It was Bates, all right, with five other men, all ranchers in the area. He knew most of them relatively well, but not well enough to call them his friends. It seemed Bates had taken far more initiative on that account than Frenchie had.

He pulled back, took a deep breath, and then stepped out, nonchalantly swinging his axe in one hand and whistling softly. He stopped, pretending to be surprised to see the men there. They were still sitting on their horses and looking around.

"Well, I'll be doggone!" Frenchie said, giving them an innocent grin. "It's my lucky day t' have the whole passel of my neighbors come t' pass the time with me. I was just thinkin' I'd sure like a good game of chess right about now, and it's just too dang far to ride to Fort Laramie."

Bates smirked. "You might not like the games we play, Frenchie, unless you're willin' t' play by our rules."

Frenchie pretended not to hear the threat in the man's words. It didn't stop him from noticing Bates wasn't mincing those words of his. It was as if he'd jumped everything up a notch overnight. "Depends what those rules are, Bates."

"I figured you'd say that," came the snide response.

"Well, now, if you don't mind, I'd just as soon skip the slippery talk and get right down to why you're here with your posse, Bates. I got the notion you ain't here for tea an' French toast."

Bates scowled. He clearly didn't like the flow of things being snatched from his hands like that. "You'll be French toast if you don't listen and listen good, Frenchie." He spat out Frenchie's name as if it was gall in his mouth.

"Oh, I'll listen." He didn't add that listening didn't mean he would pay Bates's words any mind. That would just set him to ranting and raving. Frenchie needed the man still exercising some kind of self-control so he could hear what it was he wanted.

"Good," Bates snapped. "Now, me and the other fellers, we've given you a hell of a lot of free rein over the years, an' mostly, you've kept the Indians off our backs and their hands off our stock, but it's pretty clear you've lost your charm over them now, what with all the rustlin' goin' on."

Frenchie put down the axe and folded his arms over his chest. "I held no charm over 'em. They respect me, an' I respect them."

"Well, looks like they lost their respect for you, then." Bates sneered.

"You're assumin' they're the ones stealin', but you ain't got proof."

"Who needs proof? They're doin' what all Indians do! Steal!" Bates's voice was rising in decibels and pitch.

Frenchie stared at him impassively. He didn't make any eye contact with any of the others. They had picked their spokesman. If they spoke for themselves, he'd pay them attention. Until then, he aimed to keep Bates squarely in his sights.

He couldn't trust the man as far as he could throw him. Bates was going plumb red in the face, and Frenchie wondered what Bates hated more: getting an unexpected answer from Frenchie or not getting an answer at all.

"I'm warnin' ya, Frenchie, ya better take care of those Indians, or we will."

Frenchie lifted one eyebrow. "I'll be needin' t' know exactly what your meanin' is when you say 'take care' of 'em," he said.

"You know exactly what I mean, French!" Bates snarled. "Run 'em off, get 'em out, do what ya need t' do, but do it quick, or we'll take care of your business for you, and it won't be pretty."

Frenchie shook his head. "You fellers are powerful quick on the draw," he said, this time glancing around at the rest of them. Their faces were all deadpan, half hidden beneath their hat brims, shadows thrown over their eyes. Jeff Walters, Sonny Blaine, Gill Crawford, men he'd thought were level-headed, at least, allowing themselves to be herded along by a lunatic.

He made one last-ditch effort to talk some sense into them. "How'd you like to be strung up for something before there was any kind of investigatin' into what happened an' who did it?"

"We've done all the investigatin' we need to," Bates shot back stubbornly.

Frenchie sighed. "I can't stop ya, Bates, but I sure hope you know what a heap of trouble you're startin'. There's a better way to do this, and startin' a war, ain't it."

"You've got one week," Bates replied, his eyes stony. Then he put his heels to his horse's sides and spun the animal around.

The rest of the men followed suit. They galloped off and left Frenchie staring after the dust cloud kicked up by their horses' hooves. He wished there was a way to change their minds and avoid the inevitable fight he knew was coming, but he also knew that was an impossible dream.

Chapter 9
Death in the Family

On the fourth night of her nightly vigils, Jessie was feeling the pinch. Her eyelids had drooped closed more than once, and twice, she had woken to almost falling out of the saddle. Dealing with Bates and his lot was turning out to be tougher than she'd ever imagined, but she forced herself to keep going. There was no time for slacking.

She had just shaken herself awake for the umpteenth time when the sound of hooves moving at a fast trot filled the night air. In a flash, all of Jessie's faculties were on high alert. She stayed low against Horace's neck, not wanting to stand out against a hillside or on a ridge while she listened, trying to pinpoint the direction of the sound.

The moon hung midway up in the sky, not quite full but bright enough to bathe the landscape in its pale blue light. Jessie scanned the surrounding hills. She couldn't see any cattle. They must have moved off during her last doze.

Ah, the sound was coming over the ridge to her right. She nudged Horace in the ribs, and he pricked his ears, apparently as eager for action as she was.

Going just far enough to see over the ridge, she drew Horace to a halt. The next moment, the world around her was filled with lowing, lumbering cattle and bawling calves.

Jessie sat up, certain she had stumbled across another theft. Beyond the cattle—about forty of them, not counting the calves—she could see the bulky shapes of men on horses. They wore Stetsons and high-domed Mexican-style hats. These were not likely Indians.

On impulse, Jessie grabbed her whip from the pommel horn and began laying about her, driving the cattle into a panic so that they ran, bellowing and bleating in fear as the whip cracks rang through the air like pistol shots.

A couple of curses rose over the commotion. Those were definitely not Indians. Only cowpokes could curse like that.

Jessie let them come closer, close enough to see her, before she spoke. "Funny time of day for a cowhand to be workin', don't ya think?" she yelled out at the top of her lungs. She wanted to make sure they heard every word.

"Dang you, Cattle Kate!" a voice rasped angrily. The owner of that voice rode right up to where she sat on Horace.

Her fearless mount stood his ground, blowing hard through his nostrils as he whickered and squealed a warning to the horse crowding his space.

"Should have known you were mixed up in this racket, Rafe," Jessie said, recognizing his voice more than his face, which was hidden in the shadow of his hat brim. The other men were riding closer, abandoning the scattered cattle.

"What in tarnation, Rafe?" one of them asked.

Jessie didn't recognize him, but she guessed he was working for Bates. Only that night at supper, Frenchie had told her and the others about Bates's threats. He'd mentioned it with Rafe and Wally present. Jessie had noticed something akin to satisfaction flash in Rafe's proud eyes, but it had been only a flicker, and nobody else seemed to have noticed.

"That's what I'd like t' know. Maybe Cattle Kate here can fill us in," Rafe snapped. "What are you doin' out here, woman?"

"Tryin' t' figure out what you're doin' out here," Jessie replied hotly. "But I don't hardly need anybody t' tell me. It's plain as the nose on your face, Rafe. You fellas are the rustlers, just like I figured. What's your game? Stealing folks' cows an' blaming Red Cloud's folks for it?"

"Did you hear that? She called those Indians 'folks,' as if they were just like us," another man said. His voice and his accent sounded familiar, but she couldn't place it at that moment.

"Oh, they ain't just like you. They're better," Jessie snapped back at him.

The man cursed, and the unmistakable sound of gun metal sliding against leather filled the air.

"You're on thin ice, Miss Weaver," Rafe snarled.

"I ain't miss anything. I'm Jessie," she cut in.

"You'll be dead Jessie if you don't ride out of here an' keep your big bazoo shut," Rafe said.

"You gonna shoot me?" Jessie taunted.

"No, he ain't," a horribly familiar voice said as a horse and rider stepped out of a nearby copse of cottonwoods.

"Danny! What in the blazes are you doing here?" Jessie almost wailed.

"Aw, ain't that sweet. Little brother, come t' save your hide, has he?" Rafe sneered.

"Shut up, Rafe," Danny said curtly. "And you can just slide that six-shooter of yours back in its holster, too."

Jessie's blood was past boiling. "No, keep it shucked, Rafe. Let's you and me have a duel. If I win, your cronies quit rustlin' Frenchie's cows."

Rafe burst out laughing. "An' if I win? What's the deal then?"

"You won't win." Jessie settled herself. Her blood was racing through her veins, and her muscles were twitching, ready to unholster the LeMats and do what she needed to do with them. It would be trickier than usual with such low light and with so many other armed men around, but if she could entice Rafe into a duel, she'd have only one to deal with.

"I ain't dueling no woman," Rafe spat, sliding his revolver back into its holster.

"Oh no?" Jessie countered. "You afraid I'll win? I tell ya what, I'll do what women do best an' go gossipin' to Frenchie and whoever else'll listen about what I saw here tonight."

"You didn't see nothin'." Rafe's tone was getting more and more agitated.

Jessie didn't care. She'd faced the bear so many times that poking it didn't scare her any. "I wonder what he'll do when he finds out one of his best hands is stealin' his stock."

"Jessie, we've seen what we need t' see. We can go tell Major Wood about Rafe's night shenanigans. Let the army sort this out." Danny spoke firmly but calmly.

Rafe laughed again. "The army? They won't do nothin'! They want the same thing we do. Them Indians out of the way, so us civilized folks can turn this place into more than backwoods and useless mountains."

"Civilized? If you're an example of civilized folks, well then, I guess there ain't much hope for civilization." Jessie seethed. "You mind my words, Rafe, Frenchie is goin' t' hear about this, an' so will Major Wood. Maybe the army wants the Indians out of the way, but I sure don't think they'll like the way you're fixin' t' get it done."

Without waiting for his response, Jessie wheeled Horace around and rode away. She had to admit Danny was right. There was no way for her to fix anything on her own. She'd already riled Rafe up too much with her temper and her impulsiveness. Maybe now she had caught him and the others red-handed, they'd quit their fool plans.

"You stop right there, Cattle Kate, or I swear I'll put a bullet in you." Rafe's voice grated behind her. His tone made her draw Horace to a halt. Would he do that? Put his bullet in her back while she was riding away? With witnesses? Most men, even the real outlaw types, wouldn't be caught dead shooting a woman in the back. No cowboy worth his salt liked to be called yellow livered.

A tense silence followed. Only the ragged chirping of an occasional cricket and an owl hoot could be heard while Jessie waited, holding her breath. It felt like hours she hesitated, but nothing happened. She was going to have to go with her old trick: calling the man's bluff.

As she put her heels to Horace's sides and the big horse moved forward again, his ears twitching back and forth, she heard a shout. It sounded like Danny. It sounded like he was saying something like, "No, you don't, Rafe!"

Hooves scrambled on the dirt. Two shots went off in such quick succession they almost sounded like one. A pain shot through Jessie's heart, but it wasn't a bullet. It was fear. She spun Horace back around, dreading what she'd see.

In the pale moonlight, she made out her brother's body slumped over his saddle horn, his horse side-stepping and snorting. Rafe and his friends were already hightailing it into the night.

"Danny!" Jessie cried, her legs flailing Horace's sides as she raced to her brother's side. "Danny!" she cried again, grabbing his coat sleeve and trying to lift him up, but it was useless. Instead, she grabbed his horse's reins and turned Horace's head toward Frenchie's cabin.

He might not be dead. He might be just unconscious. She hardly needed to urge Horace on. His powerful legs were already pounding the earth, gobbling up the miles, as if he knew how urgent his mission was.

When they reached the cabin, she yelled for Frenchie and Tasha. Tanner was first out of the bunkhouse, running hell for leather to her side.

"It's Danny," Jessie blurted out before he could ask. "Danny's been shot."

Tanner pulled Danny's limp form off the horse and carried him to the porch just as Frenchie opened the door, a lantern swinging in his hand, Tasha by his side. They stepped aside to let Tanner carry the young ex-dragoon indoors.

Jessie's heart was pounding in her throat as she watched her friend carry her brother into the cabin. She could hardly bring herself to go in behind them. Already the fear was crowding in on her. What if he didn't make it? Was already too late? What if she never spoke to him again?

If only she hadn't gone off half-cocked on her own mission. What had possessed him to follow her? She'd rather be dead than be the reason Danny was.

Jessie hovered on the porch, barely noticing she was wringing her hat in her hands like a dishtowel as she paced up and down, glancing at the door every time she passed it. Half a dozen times she paused, raising her hand to the doorknob, but then pulled it back and resumed pacing. What was taking so long?

The thought had barely crossed her mind as she reached the end of the porch when the sound of the door creaking open spun her around quicker than a thought. Tanner stood there, his face solemn.

"How is he?" Jessie asked tremulously, terrified of the answer but desperate to know.

"Sit down here a spell, Jess," Tanner said, his voice gentler than Jessie could ever remember hearing it.

Jessie moved toward him, hardly feeling the floorboards beneath her feet, as if in a dream. She slowly sank down into one of the rough chairs Frenchie had fashioned from tree boughs, never once taking her eyes from Tanner's face. She knew what he was going to say before he said it, but she couldn't get the words out to tell him so.

"There was nothin' we could do," Tanner said softly, looking her right in the eye. "Bullet went straight through his heart. Probably died in the saddle." His own eyes were glistening in the lantern's light he'd set down on the table before them.

Jessie was glad he spoke so frankly. She didn't want to be mollycoddled. It was a slight comfort to know Danny had gone quickly, without suffering. And yet every word stabbed mercilessly at her own heart. "He was still just a boy," she whispered, hot tears stinging her eyes.

"A boy in years, but one of the finest men I ever knew," Tanner said, his voice gruff with emotion.

Jessie glanced at him. She'd never thought about how close Tanner and Danny were, but sharing a bunkhouse night after night must have solidified their friendship. And now Danny was gone. It was an awful thought. Too sudden, too final, too avoidable. Guilt gnawed at her. "It should've been me, Tanner," she mumbled.

Tanner didn't say a word.

"He weren't supposed t' be out there."

"You weren't neither." There was no recrimination in Tanner's voice. He was simply stating a fact. "Who did it, Jessie?" he asked, a note of briskness and determination coming into his voice.

"Rafe," Jessie said simply, feeling numb. "I caught him and some other cowpokes rustlin' Frenchie's stock again. Straight up asked 'em what they were doin', an' next thing, Danny comes out of the bushes, tellin' me I should leave it to the army t' sort 'em out."

She paused. It helped to talk, helped to focus on something, try to make sense of what had just happened, if that was possible. What it didn't do was take away the heavy ache spreading like a creeping poison through every bone and muscle in her body.

"Rafe had his six-shooter out, but I figured he wouldn't shoot if I wasn't drawn yet. I turned Horace and started t' leave. I was leavin', Tanner, an' the varmint fired. Danny shouted, sayin' Rafe's name. At the same time, I heard two shots, so close they were almost one. When I turned back, Rafe an' his lot were scatterin' dirt, an' Danny was slumped over his saddle horn."

Jessie stopped again. The memory of her brother's motionless, unresponsive body was too much. She didn't want to dwell on it. The ache had spread to her throat and was all but choking her.

Tanner put an arm around her shoulder. Jessie shook, despite her efforts to control herself. She leaned against her friend, feeling suddenly weak. Then the tears came.

***

Major Wood sent some men to hold an inquest into Danny's death. The leader of the inquisition, Colonel Harry Meyer, called Jessie and Rafe into a room in Bates's large, well-furnished ranch house. Jessie was too distracted by grief and worry to wonder long about how the man's house came to be so luxuriously decorated and filled with the latest conveniences.

Jessie had remembered the voice of the man who'd sounded familiar to her. It was the soldier called Wilson, the one who had taunted her in the officer's saloon. Ned Wilson was his full name, and according to Colonel Meyer, he had left the army soon after that brief altercation.

Rafe denied there had been anybody else present, and Jessie had no other names or faces to go on.

"Would you tell the commission, in your own words, what you saw on the night in question, Miss Weaver?" Meyer opened the proceedings.

Jessie nodded and recounted the night's events in clipped, factual, concise sentences. She wouldn't let them see how deeply she was hurting. She was no weak woman. There was no way she was about to let Rafe think he'd broken her.

"Thank you, Miss Weaver. Now, you, Mr. Ives, if you please. I'd like to hear your account."

"Sure, Colonel," Rafe said, his calmness bordering on smugness that grated Jessie's nerves like a burr in a saddle blanket. "On the night in question, me and Mr. Wilson here were ridin' the range, on the lookout for wolves an' rustlers an' such. It'd been a quiet night, an' we got t' talkin'. Well, next thing we know, we've strayed over into Frenchie's grazin' lands. Lucky we did 'cause we found a passel of Mr. Bates's cows there, too. Must've strayed off from the main herd."

Jessie stared at him disbelievingly. One thing she had seen clearly in the moonlight while she was laying about with her whip was Frenchie's brand on the rumps of the cows scattering into the night. Her mind grappled for some clue where he was going with his story.

Rafe looked her straight in the eye and continued. "There we was, minding our own business, when these two riders come out of nowhere, yellin' about rustlers and wavin' their guns around. I calmed 'em down and showed 'em the brand on our cows, so Miss Weaver here turns t' leave, an' so do I. Next thing I hear Wilson callin' a warnin'. The other feller, the one who got shot, well, he's already liftin' his pistol, an' I knew if I didn't get him first, he was gonna get me, so I drew an' fired. Didn't even really aim. I just got lucky, I guess. It was him or me, Colonel Meyer, sir."

Jessie's temperature had been rising with each lying word that came out of Rafe's mouth. When he stopped speaking, she jumped to her feet, the wooden chair she sat on clattering to the floor. "Liar!" she shouted. "You're a danged liar!"

"Please, Miss Weaver, shouting won't solve anything. You've had your say. Now let him have his." The colonel was maddeningly calm.

Rafe watched her with an indulgent smile. Butter wouldn't melt in his mouth, he was so cool and collected.

"But he's lyin', Colonel," Jessie insisted.

"What about, exactly?" the colonel asked, and Jessie felt ready to shake his shoulders till his teeth rattled.

"Everything! He lied about everything!"

"Hmm…" the colonel looked down at his notes. "Let's just start with one thing at a time shall we?"

"Danny didn't draw first. It was Mr. Ives who drew first," Jessie said, glaring at Rafe and ignoring Meyer's condescending tone.

"Did you see Mr. Ives draw his gun first?" Meyer enquired.

Jessie paused. She hadn't, but she'd already told them what she'd heard Danny saying before the shots went off. Surely that showed that he'd drawn in response to Rafe drawing his gun? Did they need her to point it out to them? "I told y'all Danny shouted at Rafe before he drew. I know for a fact Danny wouldn't pull a gun on a fella without him fearin' for his life or mine. Or both."

"But you didn't actua ly see who drew first, then, did you?" Meyer went on.

Jessie wished she coulc lie, but she couldn't let herself do it. "No, sir, I didn't," she acmitted reluctantly.

Rafe looked like the cat who got the cream. It would have felt good to wipe that smirk off his face, but that also was something she would not allow herself to do, with or without witnesses present.

All she could do was wait for Rafe's lies to catch up with him. In her experience, lies usually did that. The more pressing question was whether she could sit on her hands and let blind justice do its thing. It could be a long wait.

Chapter 10
Secrets

"I can't let ya do it, Jessie," Tanner said adamantly. "You'll kill yourself at this rate."

Jessie held out her hands to him, her wrists pressed together. "You'll have t' tie me up, then, Tanner, 'cause I can't not do it."

Tanner shook his head and sighed. "You sure beat all, Jessie."

That night when Jessie left for her self-imposed nightly patrols, she had hardly gone a hundred yards when she heard hoofbeats behind her. She wheeled Horace around, her free hand ready on the butt of a LeMat when Tanner's voice reached her already burning ears in the darkness.

"Cool your heels, cowpoke. It's me," he said with a little chuckle.

"It ain't funny, Tanner," Jessie snapped, her nerves frayed to a frazzle.

"It is, and it ain't," Tanner said, his voice kind as he drew up alongside her, and they continued the ride together in silence.

Jessie wanted to send him back, but she didn't have the heart. To be honest, she was a little afraid, and Tanner's presence was a comfort. She'd never bothered herself about dying before, never feared it—and she still didn't—but she had a score to settle, and she wanted to be around long enough to do just that.

Rafe was ruthless. That much was now abundantly clear. He would stop at nothing, and he had the backing of Bates and his men. The folks on Frenchie's side had started off at a low number and had already suffered losses. Jessie needed all the help she could get, yet, she didn't want to drag Tanner into it.

"You should go back, Tanner. Get some sleep," she said, knowing he wouldn't budge but feeling like she had to say the words anyhow.

"I been gettin' enough sleep. It's you who ain't been sleepin'," he reminded her.

"Well, this is my fight, not yours."

"You sayin' I don't ride for the brand?" Tanner asked, his tone deeply tongue in cheek.

"Of course not, ya big chucklehead," Jessie shot back with a grin that Tanner probably couldn't see. His good-natured bandying about with her made her feel just that bit better.

"To split fair, though, Jess, I'll own. I'm a mite worried about ya."

"I'll be fine," Jessie insisted, though her eyelids were already drooping and her body ached.

"I sure hope so," Tanner replied. He didn't sound convinced.

Jessie shrugged it off. He'd have to live with it. That was all.

***

The next day after breakfast, while Jessie was helping wash up, Tasha looked at her long and hard. There was an almost motherly look about her as she placed her hand on Jessie's shoulder. "You are not sleeping," she said. "This is not good."

"I got things t' take care of," Jessie said, wanting to shrug off Tasha's hand but not having the heart to do it.

"You got yourself to take care of, too," Tasha said wisely.

"I'll do that when I've taken care of the other stuff," Jessie insisted stubbornly. She gave Tasha a sidelong glance as she picked up another dish and dried it. "Tanner's been at y'all about me, ain't he?"

"Tanner spoke to me and Sleeping Bear," Tasha admitted. "But our eyes told us what Tanner said long before he spoke the words."

Jessie put down the bowl and the dishcloth and leaned against the cabinet built by Frenchie's own hands. She folded her arms across her chest. "It sure means a lot to me that y'all are fussin' over me like this," she said. "But I can't sleep anyhow. Especially now that Danny..." she faltered. It was still too hard to say those words.

"Let the others help you," Tasha pleaded gently.

"They can help," Jessie said. "But they can't take my place. It's my fault what happened to Danny. I made the mess, an' I'll be danged if I leave it t' somebody else t' clean it up."

She paused, a thought occurring to her.

"Tasha, I'd have thought you, out of the lot of us, would be the one t' know what this means. Your people avenge their dead, don't they?"

Tasha nodded. "It is the way of our people. It is not the way of your people. You are not Sioux. If you kill Rafe…"

Jessie held up her hand. "I ain't fixin' t' kill him, just make sure he pays for what he's done. Rustlin' cows and blamin' your folks. I owe it to Danny to finish what we started."

Tasha replaced her hand on Jessie's shoulder. "I will not stop you, but I say you need rest. There is time for all things. There is time for vengeance, and there is time for rest."

For the rest of the day, in the intermittent moments when she was clear-headed enough to think, Jessie pondered Tasha's words. Perhaps there was another way around this. One thing she couldn't argue away was that she needed sleep.

If she thought hard enough about it, surely she'd find another way to prove what she knew about Rafe—and all the others involved in his wretched plan.

That night, she stayed in the bunkhouse, her mind running back and forth. There were others involved. She was pretty sure Bates himself was the ringleader. He'd been loud enough about his conviction that the Indians were the thieves and should be gotten rid of.

She'd confronted Rafe with the truth, and he'd lied his way out of it. Maybe if she confronted Bates, he'd get scared. Scared people, like scared animals, sometimes made fatal errors in judgment when they feared they were about to be found out. If she could just get him panicky enough to make a wrong move…

She fell asleep imagining what might happen and slept the sleep of the dead. When she woke, the sun was streaming in at the window, Tanner was gone, and she knew exactly what she was going to do.

Scrambling from her bunk, Jessie washed and dressed in a hurry and strode over to the corral with her saddle under her arm. Horace stood three-legged, lazily swatting flies with his tail, but he lifted his head and nickered as Jessie came closer.

"Fancy a little jaunt, Horace?" Jessie whispered, even though nobody else was around to hear her. She rubbed his face affectionately with her knuckles as he snorted appreciatively.

It was a good two hours' ride out to the Bates place, but it took even longer for Jessie to get there. She had to make sure Bates or his ranch hands did not see her, so her route clung to the heaviest cover, skirting ridges and hopping from one stand of trees to the next.

At last, she made it to the ridge overlooking the Bates homestead. If anybody had seen her along the way, they hadn't let her know. The homestead itself looked sleepy in the midmorning sunshine. Jessie dismounted and hunkered down beside Horace, who promptly dropped his head and began nibbling on green grass shoots.

Jessie combed the yard and the buildings with her eyes, trying to pick out anything that would give her a clue whether there were people about. In her mind's eye, she walked through the rooms of the house, trying to remember what led into what.

One good thing about the inquest being held there was that she had at least some kind of idea of the layout of the interior.

"I'll be straight with ya, Horace," she said softly. "I ain't even sure what I'm doin' here. I sure don't have a plan."

Now that she was looking at Bates's house, the reality of what she was planning hit home. She was alone. Bates would have men around who would kill for him at the drop of a hat. She couldn't just walk up to him and demand answers. Even if he gave her answers, what was she going to do with them? She needed something she could show Major Wood, and it was unlikely Bates would hand over anything like that.

No. She'd have to think of something a little more subtle. Again, she wandered through the house in her mind. Then, abruptly, she stopped. There, that room she'd walked past in the hall, with the door just slightly ajar. She'd glanced in, her thoughts wrapped up in the inquest, but the memory of what she had seen had somehow embedded itself in her brain.

It was a study. Men kept things in studies. Important things. Correspondence, letters, plans, lists, maps—so many things that could shed light on what the man of the house was up to. What if Bates was acting alone? What if he had backing from somewhere? What if Rafe was right, and the army wanted the same thing he and Bates wanted?

Jessie sat down, lying back against the bark of the box-elder that shielded her from view. She could still see the homestead below, through the gently waving branches. She pulled a piece of jerky from her jacket pocket and chewed on it, her eyes still roving back and forth over the scene below as she let her thoughts run.

Danny had shown her Mr. Mansfield's study once, when the family was out visiting, and Danny had pretended to be feeling poorly so he could stay behind with his sister. The places Mr. Mansfield had kept important documents was in his writing desk. Jessie had also known some of her employers to use a small drawer in the middle of the desk as a place to secrete away papers they wanted to shield from unworthy eyes.

That would be a good place to start. But before she could do that, she'd have to get into that study. Impossible if there were people in the house. She had seen no one go in or out in the time she'd been there, just a couple of ranch hands around the outbuildings doing necessities like mucking out stalls and feeding animals.

She glanced at the sun. It was already high in the sky, reaching eagerly for its zenith. Her eyes flickered over the buildings below once more. A movement caught her eye. It was Bates himself, emerging from his porch. He was saying something to someone behind him. Soon, a woman joined him. Jessie guessed that must be his wife. Two young boys of about ten or twelve followed her.

As Jessie watched, her chewing jaw now stilled in concentration, more people emerged from the house. They looked like ranching types, but all were decked out in their best bib and tucker, cutting a series of genteel figure if ever Jessie saw one. One man, whom Jessie recognized as Mr. Crawford from Tanner and Danny's description of him, spoke out into the warm midsummer air.

"I swear that was an inspired message, Gale," he said expansively. "Manifest Destiny is what we all should work for, like one man. It's our God-given responsibility. We can talk some more about it over Millie's fantastic cooking."

Bates said something that Jessie couldn't hear, and a smattering of laughter rose from the group, who seemed to disperse. After a while, she saw them driving out of the barn and stables in their buggies, Bates and his family taking up the rear. Jessie watched them, a sick, hollow feeling growing in the pit of her stomach.

Manifest Destiny.

She'd heard those words before, and she didn't like what they meant. Oh, there were a heap of folks who could spout off all the wonderful ideas that went with it, but the reality was far from the rosy picture they painted. She'd seen enough to convince her that Manifest Destiny was nothing more than a cooked-up term for tyranny. At least, that's how she'd seen it played out.

Treating other human beings like they were some kind of parasite, some weed that needed to be gotten out of the way so the relentless machine of so-called civilization could suck the prairies and the mountains and the rivers and the forests dry of everything that made them beautiful, everything in them that was alive.

She'd often wondered if men were trying to do God's work and making an all-fired mess of it. There didn't seem to be anything testifying to the contrary.

For a moment longer, she sat still beneath the tree. She realized it was Sunday. The gathering had obviously been a church meeting, or what Bates might have called a church meeting. The families were apparently going to enjoy Sunday lunch at another family's house. They'd be gone for the better part of the afternoon. She had all the time in the world.

Two ranch hands rode off out of the yard, one of them chatting to the other about something that seemed to animate him greatly. Jessie waited a while longer. Then, satisfied that all was quiet and deserted, she ordered Horace to stay and began her descent to the homestead.

The kitchen door was unlocked. Jessie headed for the hallway and found the room she remembered seeing on the day of the inquest. This time, the door was closed, but she found it to be unlocked, too.

Slipping inside, she closed the door behind her and glanced around the room. All the usual things were there: a bookshelf full of thick volumes and thin ones; a large desk with rolls of paper on it, probably maps; and, in the corner, the thing she'd been looking for. A writing desk.

Jessie quickly moved over to the carved wooden desk and began tugging at drawers. The one she thought might be the important one was locked. Jessie rifled through the other drawers and found a key.

With shaking fingers, a pounding heart, and ears feeling like they were pricked like a wolf's, she tried the key in the lock of the narrow middle drawer. It turned smoothly, and Jessie pulled open the drawer.

Right on top was an envelope addressed to Bates. It had already been opened, the top fold slit with some kind of knife. Jessie opened it and pulled out the paper inside. It was a letter, written in a bold yet precise hand. Jessie skimmed it, her interest growing as each word registered in her brain.

Mr. Gale Bates,

As per our discussion, I have enclosed the agreed upon down payment of $100 for your services. Let me clearly stipulate the *terms we agreed to: You will make sure the Indians are run off the land at whatever cost necessary, and you will receive the rest of the fee. You will also receive a title to a large spread of land in the Powder River Basin and the job of managing my interests on my ranch in the same area. I will pay you a monthly salary and you are free to hire whomever you believe is suitable for the job of ranch hand. Upon receiving this letter, you must destroy it. And tell no-one of our agreement, or the deal will be off.*

Mr. Richard Hastings

Jessie sucked in her breath. If anything was damning, this letter was. She began folding it up when the sound of footsteps in the house reached her ears. They were headed right down the hall toward the study, where Jessie still sat in the chair in front of the writing desk.

As quick as she could, without making an almighty racket, Jessie closed the drawer, locked it, and dropped the key back where she'd found it. Then she headed for the sash window and heaved it up. Thankfully, it slid smoothly upward, making hardly a sound. Gripping the letter in one hand, she flung one denim-clad leg over the sill, balanced for a moment, and then swung the other over before jumping off.

Landing like a cat on her toes, knees bending to reduce impact, she hunkered down, moving forward in a crouch. As she straightened up and ran, a man seemed to materialize out of thin air in front of her, and she ran right into him, knocking her wind out.

"By thunder," Rafe's gloating voice said as she sneaked the letter into her pocket, hoping he wouldn't notice. "If it ain't Cattle Kate. I never figured you for a slink."

Chapter 11
Confrontation

Tanner returned to the bunkhouse after his early morning patrol of the ranch to find Jessie's bunk empty and her saddle gone.

Silly girl probably took off lookin' for rustlers again, he thought to himself. *Pity. She would have enjoyed a breakfast with Frenchie and Tasha.*

He traipsed down to the cabin, wondering where Jessie might be riding. He hoped not too far. It was Sunday and even cowhands needed a rest. What was he thinking? Cowhands especially needed a rest, more than most folks he knew.

There wasn't much conversation at breakfast, although the food was the usual interesting combination of Sioux and English food. Tanner tucked in heartily and let himself be distracted by Chaske and Macawi's antics. Wally seemed to be engaged in the same activity, although he never was really talkative anyhow.

The little boy was feeding his sister and going to many creative lengths to get the food down her throat. Pretending to be a great stork, or an eagle, or a grizzly feeding its young, his impressions were so good, they almost distracted Macawi from the offered food.

Still, anyone realized who watched that she was enjoying every moment. She often chewed and swallowed a mouthful without even realizing she had opened her mouth.

"Y'all mind if I take some along for Jessie when she gets back?" Tanner asked when the meal was over.

"Sure thing," Frenchie replied without hesitation. "But why don't you sit a while longer? You too, Wally. We ain't in no hurry today."

Tanner paused. It would be good to spend some time in an actual house, maybe play a game of cards or two without gambling, talk about anything but the current affairs in the area. "I reckon it won't hurt none if I do," he accepted.

Frenchie motioned him and Wally through to the living area while Chaske jumped up, eager to do the washing up. He hated drying.

"Jessie been getting any sleep?" Frenchie asked before they had even sat down.

"Far as I know, she was there all last night. At least, she was still in her bunk when me and Wally left for our rounds this morning. Not sure where she is now, though. Bunk's empty and saddle's gone."

"I never saw a body work like that one," Wally said, shaking his head as he lit his pipe. "It's like she's got the blue blazes drivin' her night an' day."

"Somethin' like that," Tanner replied.

"Well, it sure is good to know she's been gettin' some shut eye at least," Frenchie remarked. "I ain't in the habit of workin' my hired hands into the ground, but I'll be danged if I know how t' make her stop."

"You an' me both, Frenchie," Tanner said wryly.

"You fellers in the mood for a game of chess?" Frenchie offered, going to fetch his hand-carved set from the rustic sideboard against the wall. Instead of the usual pawns, kings, castles, and knights, it consisted of warriors, chiefs, tipis, and buffalo. Tanner welcomed the distraction.

It was hours later, when they had finished their third coffee, that he felt antsy about Jessie. Surely she should have come in again by now? She would have guessed the rest of them might be at the cabin. It was already a tradition for the hands to visit with their employer, something Tanner was not accustomed to but appreciated.

"Hey, Wally. How about you take over from me here? I've a mind t' check up on Jessie. Make sure she's eatin'."

Wally, who was dozing on a buffalo robe, stirred and yawned. He opened one eye and looked at Tanner. "I ain't much for chess, but I'll do it. Give Frenchie a chance to win some," he chuckled.

Tanner laughed and stepped outside, making his way quickly to the bunkhouse. It was still empty. Jessie's saddle was still gone. Tanner strode out to the corral. Horace wasn't there. He felt more than a little antsy. Could she have run into the rustlers again? Had they shot her this time? Rafe had got off really easy the last time. Usually, that gave a fellow enough nerve to try a second stunt.

Agitation kept his tired mind whirling. He knew her route. He'd been with her on it before, so he could easily ride it to check if she was there or if there were any signs of a scuffle, a shooting. But would she take the same route again? It was a risk he had to take. He returned to the cabin where Wally and Frenchie were in the middle of their game.

"I'm goin' out t' check on Jessie's route," Tanner said without preamble. "She ain't in the bunkhouse, an' Horace ain't in the corral. Sun's almost halfway across the sky. She should've been back by now."

Wally looked up at him, his eyebrows knotting together in the middle. "We're comin' too," he said.

"One of us ought t' stay here with Tasha and the young'uns," Tanner said as Frenchie's wife looked up from her weaving, her eyes dark with concern. "After what Rafe pulled off, I ain't comfortable leavin' nobody alone."

Frenchie nodded. "If you fellers ain't back before two hours are up, we'll ride down to the Blaine ranch an' get help."

Tanner wanted to say they might be better off riding out to the Sioux village to ask for help, but decided against it. Instead, he left silently with Wally in tow.

They rode the full length of Jessie's usual route, even took some detours into small canyons and gullies that looked like they might hide something, but their search came up fruitless. All they found were a few cows looking for shelter from the hot midday sun.

"I know she's liable t' be pretty unpredictable, but it ain't like her t' stay away from mealtimes," Tanner muttered, his eyes still scanning the surrounding hillsides even while he and Wally made their way back to Frenchie's cabin.

"I ain't known her as long as you have, but I'd say that's about right," Wally agreed.

Everything in Tanner he d him back from giving up. There had to be a way to find her. He couldn't just go back to the cabin and rely on the other ranchers. After what Frenchie had told them about Bates arriving on his doorstep and demanding that he take care of the "thieving Indians," he couldn't see how they'd get any cooperation from the ranchers who had stood by Bates.

If their suspicions were right and Bates was, in fact, spearheading the cattle rustling, then it was more likely they'd had a hand in her disappearance. Tanner knew from experience, though, that it would do no good to confront them and ask them outright, unless he had some kind of proof. On an impulse, he decided there was one last place they could look.

"You go on ahead to the cabin, Wally. Tell Frenchie we ain't found her. I'll ride on out to Red Cloud's village, see if she's there."

"I sure hope she is," Wally said encouragingly before he put his spurs to his horse's sides and drew ahead of Tanner.

Tanner turned Trigger's head to the northwest and spurred him to a fast canter. "You and me, both, Wally. You and me both," he said under his breath. He might be mad at her for making them fret for nothing, but his anger would only last a short while before his relief overwhelmed it. He hadn't ever really pondered what it might be like not to have Jessie around. Now he knew why. The thought was just too doggone awful.

It took him a while to find the village—they'd moved about five miles west since the last time he'd been there— and when he approached, his presence aroused a commotion he hadn't expected.

Young children who had been playing on the outskirts of the village saw him first. They ran shrieking into the center of the sprawl of tipis, waving their arms and pointing back in his direction.

Tanner slowed Trigger to a walk and raised both hands away from his sides, holding them high in the air but still gripping the reins. He'd have to tread carefully. They didn't know him the way they knew Jessie. His mouth went dry, and his palms sweat. If he could only get close enough for Red Cloud to recognize him.

To his dismay, a crowd of young men, emerging from their tipis, headed straight for their grazing horses and vaulted onto the animals' bare backs. In the distance, Tanner couldn't see if they were armed, but it was safe to bet they were. To the teeth, probably.

That was one thing about the Sioux. They left nothing to chance with protecting their own.

He kept on plodding closer, his arms growing tired, pins and needles pricking at his fingers and wrists, but he dared not drop them an inch. The young men were galloping closer, some of them already whooping a war cry. Tanner's heart was beating in his throat, the rhythm echoing in his ears.

They came close enough that he could see the look of distrust and warning on their faces. The prayers he had been praying in his mind became whispered pleas on his lips.

Suddenly, one man wheeled his horse around and gave a sharp command in Sioux. Tanner did not know what it was, but the effect was instant. The riders all yanked their horses to a dust-scattering halt. The man rattled off some more Sioux words, and Tanner heard Jessie's name.

Relief washed over him in hot and cold waves. Half of the men spun their horses around and headed back to the village at a gallop. The rest surrounded him as the man who had called halt advanced confidently toward Tanner. He was still holding up his hands, just to be sure.

"You friend of she who works like a man, no?"

It took a while for Tanner to realize he was talking about Jessie. The woman who did a man's work. He'd forgotten how she'd told him about the native way of naming people based on their habits or their achievements. It was interesting that Red Cloud's name had not changed during his lifetime. He'd been born under a scarlet morning sky, and that was a sign of great destiny.

"Yes, I am her friend. My name is Tanner," he replied, recognizing him as the man who had translated for Red Cloud when he and Jessie had met with the chief in Crazy Woman Canyon. "She is missing. We can't find her. I came here to look for her."

"You come," the man said, his face and eyes inscrutable. He swung his horse around, and Tanner followed along behind. The surrounding men kept pace, continuing to form a ragged but resolute living corral around him and Trigger. They were clearly giving their opinions of him—remarks followed by sniggers and snorts of laughter.

Tanner kept his eyes on the horseman in front of him. He didn't recall everything Jessie had told him about the ways of the Lakota, but one thing that had struck a chord with him was that they honored those who showed no fear or agitation.

It wasn't an easy ask. Tanner's first instinct was to look around him, to see the looks on their faces. To know if those were mocking or merely lighthearted remarks being made.

Instead, he pretended he couldn't even hear them. They had almost reached the village when someone said something in a low voice and they emitted a few ahs and ohs in muted, almost awed tones.

"We take you to Maȟpíya Lúta," the leading man said over his shoulder as they entered the village. A far quieter and fearful reception greeted him compared to the one Jessie and Tasha had received. Children hid behind their mother's deerskin skirts, peeping out with wide black eyes. Women and old men whispered to each other, as if he could even understand what they were saying.

The other horsemen had apparently alerted their chief to his coming. When they rounded a tipi, Red Cloud stood, arms folded, in front of his lodge. He signed something. Tanner could just make it out from what he'd learned from Jessie.

What do you want, white man?

The man led him right up to the Sioux leader and motioned to Tanner to dismount. He did so and went to stand in front of Red Cloud. "Howdy do, Chief Red Cloud. I'm looking for Jessie. She's missing. Since this morning."

Red Cloud snapped something in Sioux. He clearly wasn't about to make things easier for Tanner.

"You think she is here? You think we hurt her?" the translator said with almost the same intensity.

Something else Jessie had taught him was that it was better never to answer in the negative. Never contradict him. That is rude. Rather, offer an alternate truth. "She trusts you. She picked up some trouble with some other folks. I figured she might come here for help."

A glimmer of appreciation shone in Red Cloud's eyes without his interpreter translating a single word. He spoke in slow, deliberate syllables, the sternness in his face almost imperceptibly softened. "Strong Woman, not here," the translator said. "But we can help her friend to find her."

He turned to face the men who were still gathered around, some of them mounted, some of them leaning against their horse's shoulders or rumps, all staring at Tanner with unabashed curiosity. A flood of rapid words poured from his mouth, and almost instantaneously, two men, still casually sitting on their horses, nodded and gestured, while responding in rapid Sioux.

The translator nodded and grunted in response as he listened closely, chipping in now and then with what sounded like questions. Then he turned his attention back to Tanner. His words pierced Tanner's mind like a bullet. "They say they see her on the mountain behind the lodge of the Bates man."

"Bates? Gale Bates?" Tanner stammered.

"Yes. She sit and watch the lodge. She alone. My friends leave. They do not stay around there long. Bates lodge not safe for Sioux. Bates like to shoot first before ask questions."

"How long ago was that?"

"Middle of the day," came the reply. "Sun up there." The translator pointed to the sky's zenith.

Tanner almost forgot the other things Jessie had taught him. Never leave abruptly, even if there's an emergency.

Always state where you're going and why you're leaving. "I got t' go there," he said, swinging back up into the saddle. "I got t' find her. Bates'll shoot her soon as look at her. He likes her less than he likes you folks, if you can believe that."

Red Cloud barked a command. Tanner looked into the chief's eyes as his men scattered. He could have sworn they held a look uncannily like a proud father's.

"Maȟpíya Lúta say you take warriors with you," the interpreter said.

Tanner bowed his head as Trigger trod hot bricks beneath him, clearly sensing his sudden change of mood. "I sure am powerful honored," he said, "but this is something I got t' do alone." He didn't tell them so, but he worried all hades would break loose if he rode onto the Bates ranch with a posse of Sioux warriors. That was exactly the thing they were all trying to avoid.

Red Cloud nodded and waved one hand in a stately arc. The glimmer of a smile crossed his lips as he barked another command, and the men gathered once more around his tipi. Then he spoke in a deep, soft tone.

"Maȟpíya Lúta says, 'May the Mysterious Spirit be with you, he who loves his friend.'"

Tanner heard the translator's words, but he had trouble internalizing them. He doffed his hat, spun Trigger around on a dime, and let the horse have his head, using only enough rein to guide him in as straight a line as possible toward the Bates ranch. The chances she was still there were almost nil. But he had to know.

Heaven help the man if he had done anything to hurt Jessie. Tanner would make sure he paid six ways from Sunday.

When he reached the Bates homestead, the sun hung low on the horizon and it lathered his horse in sweat. Bates and his family were enjoying an al fresco supper out on their back porch. Tanner didn't care.

He strode right up to the man, removed his hat, nodded a cursory greeting to Mrs. Bates, and folded his arms over his chest. "I heard tell Jessie was here at your place around noon today," he said without preamble, "and now she's missin'. Where is she?"

Bates looked up at him slowly as he reached for the napkin on his lap and deliberately wiped his mouth. "Never mind this rude feller," Bates said to his family. "You enjoy your supper. I'll take care of him." With that, he rose and gripped Tanner's arm just above the elbow.

Tanner yanked himself free and glared at the man, but he followed him over to the barn where Tanner stopped outside. "We can talk here, where your folks can see us," he said. "It's far enough so they can't hear what we're sayin', if you've got somethin' t' say that ain't meant for your boys' ears."

"I ain't sure what got into ya, bargin' in on my family's supper, and I sure as hell don't know where your precious Jessie is or who told ya she was here," Bates snapped in a hoarse whisper.

"Some Sioux fellas told me they saw her here around noon. Up on the mountain behind your place. She ain't been home since mornin'."

Bates snorted derisively, then he trained two mean, glittering eyes on Tanner. "You're believin' a couple of savages over your own kind?" he asked rhetorically.

Tanner glowered back. "Well, long as my kind is going back on their own promises an' lyin' about how folks got shot, I guess all the folks I can trust is the fellas you call savages. The ones who know how t' keep their word."

Sparks shot from Bates's eyes as his voice reverted to a low growl. "You'd better get off my land, Nugent, before I put a bullet in your ever-lovin' skull."

Chapter 12
Frustration

Frenchie removed his hat and worriedly rubbed the bald patch on the back of his head as he stared at his herd in the holding pen. There were another ten cattle missing that morning. The morning after Jessie had gone missing. Things were getting out of hand, and he felt powerless. It seemed Bates and his men, if they were the ones stealing the cattle, as Jessie suspected, were intent on starting a war, no matter what it cost them.

Myself, I'd just as soon move out somewheres else, if it weren't for Tasha's folks wanting her near. Wally stood beside him. He seemed to carry the same dark cloud in his thoughts. Tanner was still out scouring the hillsides for any sign of Jessie or even Horace. Where Horace was, Jessie was bound to be. The horse followed her around like he was her shadow.

Frenchie was still wallowing in despondency when the sound of hoofbeats made him and Wally look at each other as if they'd rehearsed it. Then, as one man, they turned toward the the sound. Tasha stood up on the porch, dropping her weaving. She quickly told Chaske to take his sister inside, and the boy immediately obeyed. Moments later, a posse of horsemen crested the rise and rode right up to where Frenchie and Wally stood.

Frenchie figured he should have known it would be Bates leading them. He sighed inwardly. If only he could chase them all away with a few rifle shots into the air. But that would only add fuel to Bates's fire, so Frenchie resisted the temptation. "Anything I can do for you folks?" he asked instead as Bates dismounted and came to stand right in front of him. The man's stance was belligerent, challenging.

"Yeah, there is," Bates snapped. "You can get those Indians off the land. I don't know who they think they are, keepin' it all for themselves and their brats. I told ya, keep 'em in check, but they've gone an' taken thirty head of Jeff Walters's best cows."

Frenchie folded his arms across his chest, aware that Tasha stood slightly behind him. She probably had the rifle hidden behind her deerskin dress. "Hmmm... I've lost me a packet of ten," Frenchie said, stroking his mustache. I was fixin' t' ride out to Red Cloud's village an' ask if he knows aught about it." He didn't tell Bates he hadn't been planning to do any such thing until the troublemaker had appeared over the rise.

"No, you won't," Bates shot back angrily. "We've been waitin' on you long enough, and you ain't delivered no how. We're goin' out there ourselves. To get back our cows and teach those thievin' Indians a lesson they won't forget in a hurry. And when we've got shed of these varmints, you'll have t' give up your squaw an' start livin' like a real white man."

Frenchie sighed and looked over at Wally. Wally shrugged. Frenchie looked back at Bates. "I told ya before. I'll tell ya again: you ain't got the foggiest what you're dealin' with. Besides, you still ain't got proof they took your cows or anybody else's."

"An' I told you before, I got all the proof I need," came the stubborn reply. "You got one last chance t' join with your own race an' take the land that's rightfully ours."

"Rightfully ours?" Frenchie echoed, thinking the man must have completely taken leave of his senses.

"Don't tell me you ain't heard of Manifest Destiny, Baltimore French," Bates said mockingly.

"Oh, I've heard of it," Frenchie replied grimly. "I just put little store by it. Sounds like a couple of words someone put together t' make folks do what they want them to do."

Bates stared at him, clearly uncomprehending.

"Never could get it straight in my mind how Manifest Destiny meant a man could take something that ain't his. I always figured that was something for a just an' righteous God t' do. Not greedy folks lookin' t' take whatever they can get without givin' nothin' back."

Bates went red in the face and lunged at Tasha, as if he wanted to snatch her away.

Frenchie stepped between them, chopping Bates's arm hard in the bend of his elbow, so he released Tasha's wrist. "Try a trick like that again and I'll let my wife show you some tricks she knows with a rifle," he growled, hoping Bates could see the fire flashing in his eyes.

Bates stepped back, a shadow of fear crossing his face, then the anger sparked in them again. "Let's go, fellers," he said to the men behind him, his eyes still trained malevolently on Frenchie and Tasha. "When we're done, we can always come back and take care of this here traitor an' his squaw an' his half-breeds."

None of the men replied.

Bates swung into the saddle and dragged his horse's head around to the left. "This ain't the last you've seen of me, French. You've got five days t' change your mind. Five days," he said in passing before his horse galloped off, kicking up sod and rocks as it went.

The other ranchers followed, none of them speaking a word, none of them looking Frenchie in the eyes.

Frenchie watched them go. Then he turned to his hired hand. "Wally, go find Tanner and tell him we need t' warn Major Wood of Bates's plans. The army said they'd protect the Indians from fellers who's fixin' t' hurt 'em. Let's see 'em put their money where their mouth is."

Wally grunted an affirmative and headed straight to the horse corral as Frenchie put his arm around Tasha's shoulders.

"You knew I had the rifle?" she asked.

"Of course. I know you," he replied, his belly still burning with rage at the thought of Bates's claw on her wrist. "Bates is turnin' into a loose cannon, though. An' I don't know we can trust the army t' keep their promises."

Tasha's eyes grew dark with concern. "You are worried about my people?"

"Not for what Bates'll do to 'em but for what every other rancher, settler, and army man from here t' the Black Hills will do to all your people when they give Bates what he's got comin' to him."

Tasha nodded silently and rested her head on his shoulder. He didn't need to ask her if she understood.

***

Two days of hard riding later, with two spare horses and only a couple of hours stopping at night, Tanner approached Major Wood's office at a shambling trot. He knew he looked awful, and he hoped the sight of him would shake the major up enough to listen to him. His disheveled appearance and the lather on his horses drew more than a few curious looks, but Tanner pretended not to see them, keeping his eyes hidden behind the brim of his hat.

He stepped up to the door and hammered the brass knocker assertively. The voice that answered was tired and sounded a little cranky.

Tanner sucked in his breath and then exhaled as he pushed the door open and stepped into the office. "It's a fine mornin', Major," Tanner said, removing his hat as he did so.

"Yes. It was until you disturbed me…" Major Wood looked up and left his sentence unfinished. "What in the hell happened to you, man?"

"I left Crazy Woman Canyon two days ago," Tanner informed him.

"I can't see why you live in a place with a name like that," Major Wood muttered, his eyebrows meeting in a frown.

"It ain't me that's crazy," Tanner replied. "It's that Gale Bates. He's herded together a posse for himself an' they're threatenin' to chase out the Indians from the Powder River Basin. Says they're stealin' cows. But he ain't got…"

"Yes, yes, I know," Wood cut him short. "So, why are you here?"

Tanner stared at the man, wondering if he was drunk or just stupid. "The treaty our government made with the Indians. It says the army'll protect 'em if United States folks try to hurt 'em, drive 'em off their land."

Wood sighed heavily and relit a half-smoked cigar. He shook his head. "I don't have men available for that," he said, not making eye contact with Tanner.

Tanner set his hat down on the desk and leaned on the polished wooden surface with both hands so his face was on a level with the major's. "That's a great thumpin' lie, and you know it," he said emphatically.

Wood let out a "Humph!" and lifted his face to stare back at Tanner with a brave show of indignation that Tanner saw right through. For a few minutes more, they stared at each other, Wood clearly trying to stare the cowhand down, but Tanner wasn't about to budge.

At last, Wood looked down at his smoldering cigar. "I can't help you," he said simply. "Bates might not go through with his threats. Until he does, we can't do anything about it."

"So that's the way it is, is it?" Tanner said, not caring if the major knew what he meant. He straightened up and pressed his hat firmly back on his head. "Well, I guess I'll just have t' drum up some help myself, won't I?"

He marched back out through the door and headed straight for the bachelor officers' quarters. His head hurt and he was thirsty, but he couldn't bother about that just yet. There was a bigger mission waiting for him. "You fellas uphold the treaties of your government, do ya?" he asked rhetorically at the top of his lungs.

A few soldiers up on the top balcony of Old Bedlam peered down and began whispering among themselves.

"Well, how about you do what they said you would do and protect the Indians from rancher folks whose taken it in their heads to drive those tribes off their land that the government gave 'em? How about you do what's right? How many of you have the guts t' stand by the fella who's innocent without lookin' at the color of his skin?"

Men were peering through the windows of the lower floor of Old Bedlam. Some stepped outside to get a look at the stranger challenging them. Curious children ran out of their houses and down to the parade ground to see what was going on, some with their mothers tripping along behind, trying to get them to go back into the house, where it was safe.

"Are there any men of honor in this fort? Or is it all about your danged so-called Manifest Destiny? Take what you want an' don't give a continental for the folks who's been here longer than any of us?"

One by one, the faces disappeared from the windows, the soldiers on the porch and the balcony melted back into the buildings. The children's mothers grabbed their arms and led them away, shushing their protestations. A middle-aged man in a neatly pressed civilian suit, his slicked-back dark brown hair already showing signs of graying, stepped out of the officer's bar and directly up to Tanner. His eyes were deep blue and communicating understanding, but also a strange sort of condescension. It caught Tanner off guard. The man smiled, the crow's feet at the corners of his eyes deepening. "You're wasting your time, son," he said in a velvety bass voice. "Let's you and me take a walk out on the parade ground."

Tanner felt confused. He'd come there for help, and the men who were supposed to help were turning their backs on him. Now this stranger wanted to take a walk with him on the parade ground? Still, something in Tanner cautioned him to listen to what the man had to say. At least it gave him time to regroup his thoughts. The man led Tanner along, his hand guiding Tanner by the elbow.

"You want these men to fight against their own kind? Do you honestly think they'd do that? Fight against the ranchers on the side of hostile Indians to protect the land they claim is theirs. But where is their claim? They've built nothing, settled nothing. The land is wild. Just like them. Wild and hostile."

Tanner stopped, pulling his arm free from the man's grip. "Hostile, you say?" he replied, staring into the man's eyes. "Now, you tell me, mister, do you honestly think they don't see us as the hostiles, comin' into their territory, killin' off all the game they've been survivin' on for hundreds of years, an' tellin' 'em where they can an' can't set up their villages?"

"You're the only one around here who sees it that way, son," the man said, shrugging his shoulders.

"My handle's Tanner Nugent, and I ain't your son," Tanner snapped, incensed at the stranger in his eastern garb. "Who might you be anyhow, figurin' you know so much about things out here?"

"The name's Richard Hastings, from Boston," the man said, holding out his hand.

Tanner looked at the offered hand and kept his hanging by his sides. It was all he could do not to clench them into fists. "I'd be careful how I talk about Indians bein' hostile an' not ownin' nothin' and all. Folks might figure you're part of the problem," Tanner said slowly, watching for the man's response.

Richard Hastings simply laughed. "Because I come from the city?" he asked with an amused smirk. "You can't outrun progress, Mr. Nugent. It's unrelenting and powerful. Savagery has to bow before it some time or another. You'll see."

"Oh, I saw all I need to," Tanner responded before turning on his heel and marching straight back to the major's office. This time, he entered without knocking first.

"What do you mean by this?" Major Wood looked up from the map he was studying, his eyes flashing.

"I mean to tell ya it ain't right, lettin' a city fella tell y'all what to do," Tanner said hotly, once again planting his palms on the major's desk. "You ought t' be honorin' that treaty our government signed, not listenin' to the say-so of some stranger from Boston."

Major Wood stood to his feet, towering over Tanner. Tanner straightened up, too. He wasn't as tall as the major, but he wasn't under his command, either. There was no way he was going to let the army man intimidate him.

"Get ahold of yourself, man," Major Wood barked, although he seemed to struggle a little to keep control of himself. He lowered his voice. "I know what the treaties say.

You think I don't lie awake nights, wondering which is the lesser evil and not knowing how to choose? If I send my men out there to fight against the ranchers, I'll bet an entire year's salary that more than half of them'll end up fighting for the ranchers. And then we'll really have a war on our hands."

The major paused and wiped a hand across his sweating brow.

"I have to hope Bates'll back down on his threats. If he doesn't, I have to hope his little escapade will fail. And if it does, where does that leave us? With more reasons for white men to attack Indians? More war? I'm under strict instructions from the president to avoid war with the Indians in the Powder River Basin at all costs. It's certainly no picnic, man. Let me tell you that."

Tanner held the major's gaze for a few moments. "I reckon if a government makes a promise, its officers ought t' carry it out," he intoned. "There's goin' t' be a war anyway, eventually. Stoppin' it ain't your job. Upholdin' the law is. Honorin' treaties is. Keepin' US citizens in line. That's your job."

Without another word, Tanner turned and left. He'd done what he could. He'd relayed the information to the major. What Woods did with it was his responsibility. Tanner watered his horses, walked them up and down the parade ground a little, bought a meal of stew from an emigrant wagon train and lit out again, back to Crazy Woman Canyon.

There was still one more thing he could do. He could join Frenchie and the Indians in stopping the knuckleheaded ranchers who were bent on unleashing all Hades on themselves and everyone around them.

And he had to find Jessie.

Please, God, if you're there, keep her safe.

He didn't dare give voice to the fear that his prayer might be too late.

Chapter 13
Branded

The first thing Jessie noticed was her own coughing. Her throat felt dry and scratchy. The stifling smell of dust clung to her nostrils. She tried to snort it out, but that only ended up with more dust floating around. Her eyes flickered open, and she realized a dull ache throbbing in her head.

All she could see were dimly lit, dusty floorboards. She was lying face down on them, her hands tied behind her back, her shoulders aching, her hands numb.

Jessie groaned as she rolled over onto her side and looked up at the rafters above her. Every inch of her ached. For a moment she lay still, catching her breath and fighting off the feeling of nausea rising in her stomach. Then she peered around.

Her prison seemed to be an old ramshackle cabin. Some firewood lay stacked beside a woodstove behind her. A broken cup without an ear sat on the stove. Other than that, the cabin seemed to be bare.

Daylight filtered in through the boarded-up windows, but not enough for Jessie to tell what time of day it was. She tried to move her feet, but they were also tied together.

A cough and the turning of a page startled her, and she lurched to her knees, searching for the source of the sound.

There, in a corner beside the stove on a bench covered with newspaper, sat a man decked out in city clothes.

He was reading a large newspaper and didn't seem to notice her presence or the fact she had moved. He looked familiar, and she could only guess she'd seen him at the fort some time or other when she'd been there with Frenchie. What was familiar was her gun belt with its contents lying beside him on the cabin floor.

"Hey, mister," she said. "Who in tarnation are you, an' why am I trussed up like a Thanksgivin' turkey?"

"You can call me Hastings," the man replied without looking up. "We're keeping you here till we decide what to do with you. You might come in handy."

Jessie stared at him, her irritation rising higher than her fear. "Come in handy? You ain't makin' no sense, Mister Hastings," she snapped.

"Oh, ain't I?" he mocked, giving her a look of disdain. "How about this: What were you doing in Gale Bates's house yesterday? That make any sense to you?"

At his words, the memories came flooding back. Taking the letter from Bates's writing desk, jumping out the window and running bang into that coyote, Rafe.

She wondered if they knew she'd read it. For a few moments, her mind whirled, trying to remember what she'd read in the letter, while Hastings went on reading his paper. She'd have to play this smart.

"You're tellin' me it's illegal to pay a neighbor a visit?" she quipped, shifting over to the stove so she could lean against it. Standing on her knees wasn't all that comfortable, but sitting on her feet would be even worse.

Hastings was chuckling to himself. Whether at what she'd said or something he'd read in the newspaper, she couldn't tell. Then his eyes went cold, and he looked up at her. "What did you find in the study?"

So there it was.

"Nothin' much," Jessie lied. "I was hopin' t' land me some chink, but I lucked out. Can't figure out where Bates keeps his dimes. He must have plenty of 'em, considerin' his spread and all the hands he hires. Fella like that ain't doin' too poorly for himself. You'd figure he'd have some stashed away somewhere. Maybe I should've slashed open his mattress."

She was babbling intentionally. She had to make this Hastings fellow think she was a simple thief who didn't care what he knew. What she was trying to figure out in the back of her mind was where she'd heard his name before and why a fancily dressed city dandy would hold her hostage after Rafe had caught her out.

Hastings's eyes narrowed. He appeared to be trying not to believe her. She wondered what Rafe had told him about her accusations against Bates and Rafe. Jessie decided it wasn't a good idea to let him think too long. She launched into another monologue.

"That Bates fella, now he's a smart one, and no mistake. Smarter than most folks might think at first sight."

Hastings chuckled again, his eyes drifting back to his newspaper. "That's a thinly veiled insult if ever I heard one," he smirked.

Jessie wondered if he didn't think Bates was smarter than he looked, but she went on as if he hadn't spoken. "I reckon he'll have the biggest spread sooner or later. Probably end up buyin' out all the others."

Hastings looked up at her, his eyes once more narrowed to little slits. "You aren't too far off the money, miss," he said, looking smug. "Bates might not look too smart, but he's a fair bit smarter than the rest of the hillbillies out here. Won't be long before he's the richest of the lot, too, with the biggest spread."

The dawning of a revelation blossomed in Jessie's mind. *Hastings!* Someone called Richard Hastings had signed that letter! This had to be the man. The last thing she wanted to do was make him think she was aware of his scheming with Bates. Yet, something in her wanted to hear him make the confession.

"Well, yeah, I can see how a body might think that," Jessie commented as if she were merely thinking out loud. "I'll be danged if I can figure how he's going to do it, though. The way things are lookin' now, those Indians ain't goin' t' budge from the Powder River Basin. Best grazin' is out there, plumb all the way over to the Black Hills. I reckon a fella will have t' be mighty good at drivin' deals to graze his beeves on their lands. Them Sioux are a hard sell on a good day."

Hastings looked over his newspaper. Jessie's heart stood still. "You sure you found nothing in Bates's study?" he asked.

Jessie shook her head emphatically. "No, sir. Man's a skinflint. Smart enough to hide his dough where nobody can find it." She paused. "There any missin'? Is that why you fellas trussed me up and tossed me in here?"

Hastings didn't reply, simply looked at her with eyes that seemed a million miles away.

Jessie didn't like the silence. She felt compelled to fill it. "I swear, I lucked out. There was nothin'. You can check my pockets if you ain't done it already."

Hastings looked back at her, a slightly horrified expression on his face. In that moment, she remembered shoving the letter into her pocket when Rafe grabbed her. Had they seen it? Taken it? Was it still there?

She had no way of knowing, and she couldn't check with him watching her. With her heart beating in her throat, she focused on her captor again.

"Do you take me for a common thug?" Hastings said. "To conduct a body search on a woman?"

"I can do the searchin' for ya, if you'll cut these ropes around my wrists," Jessie offered generously, not thinking the city man would take the bait but electing to try anyhow.

For a few moments, Hastings sat looking at her, apparently weighing the situation in his mind. What exactly he might consider, Jessie could only wonder. To her surprise, his next actions seemed to show he trusted her, or perhaps he thought a mere woman could do nothing to outsmart him.

"All right." Hastings put down his paper and got up. Walking the few steps over to where Jessie knelt, he pulled a knife from his jacket pocket that didn't look like it belonged to him. "Hold still," he said brusquely, gripping her lower arm.

Jessie obeyed and felt the rawhide around her wrists go slack as he sawed through them. She timed her moment carefully, eyeing out the nearest heavy piece of firewood lying at her calf.

As soon as her right hand was free, she reached down and grabbed the branch. Swinging it around, she twisted her torso to put maximum force behind the wood and connected as hard as she could with Hastings's temple, just as he straightened up.

Most likely, he didn't even see it coming before it hit him and his eyes glazed over. He staggered backward, teetered for a moment, then pitched forward. Jessie, still on her knees, caught him before he broke his nose on the floorboards.

"Don't know what Rafe or Bates were thinkin', leavin' a city boy to watch me," she muttered to herself. She quickly untied her ankles and then transferred the rawhide to her captor's wrists and ankles. She looked down at his sleeping form.

"Sorry I had t' do that to ya, Mr. Hastings, but you sort of had it comin', anyhow," she whispered, shoving her hand into her pocket. The letter was still there. She pulled it out, gave it one long look, collected her guns from beside the bench, and stepped outside.

It was early afternoon. Who knew how long the others had been searching for her. But that wasn't her first concern. She had to let the other ranchers know what Bates was up to.

Now that she'd seen how closely he and Hastings were working together, she wondered if any of them had any idea. Surely Bates wouldn't want to have too many others in on the deal. That would only make his share smaller.

She stayed close to the cabin for a while, scouting around for signs of an outside watchdog, but found nothing. Bates really wasn't smarter than he looked.

On an impulse, she gave a long, piercing whistle, ending it with a trill and a scoop up to a higher pitch. A shrill whinny reached her ears only seconds later, and Horace came crashing through the underbrush.

"You'll give us both away, you great galumphing elephant," Jessie laughed into the horse's mane as he rubbed his cheek against her shoulder.

It took a while to find out where she was, but soon enough, using the highest peaks around to orient herself, she made her way down to Bates's ranch. Bates wasn't there. Neither were any of his hired hands. Jessie sneaked into the house for a second time to find Mrs. Bates in the drawing room with her two sons. All three were reading.

Jessie pulled out her LeMats, intentionally dragging the sights against the leather of the holsters. The three looked up, startled. Mrs. Bates gave a little scream. Bates really was stupid or overconfident.

"You," Jessie said, pointing the LeMat in her right hand at the nearest boy. "Tie up your ma and your brother. Use them bow things on the curtains."

The young man, his eyes wide with fright, did as he was told. Jessie made sure he tied the knots tight, using her LeMats as an incentive. Then she tied up the boy himself and strode off to Bates's study.

She took her time. Bates was clearly taking fewer precautions now that he thought he had her hogtied in an old cabin. She searched through all the documents she could find, looking for anything that looked like it could point a finger at Bates.

At last satisfied she'd gathered all the evidence she needed, Jessie shoved everything into her saddlebag and went back to the trio in the drawing room. One boy was crying. The mother was doing her best to calm him, but she sounded pretty unsettled herself.

"Are you goin' t' kill us, miss?" the other boy asked, his eyes begging for mercy as she stepped over to the settee she'd sat them upon.

Jessie stopped and folded her arms across her chest. "What do you figure, sonny boy?" she asked.

The boy's lip quivered and his brother's wailing intensified, along with the frantic shushing from his mother.

Jessie closed her eyes and took a deep breath. "If you're thinkin' I'm anythin' like your father or his hired hands, you've got another think comin'," she said shortly. "I'll be cuttin' y'all loose an' hightailin' out of here. You better count to five hundred before you move your sorry behinds from this settee, y'hear me?"

All three of them nodded.

"Good. No hanky-panky. I'll be watchin' my nine o' clock. You can betcha."

She could tell by their faces they believed her. Without another word, she left, striding quickly out to the waiting Horace and scattering dirt like all the hounds of hell were after her.

The sign from Bates and his men was easy to follow. There must have been about twenty or thirty horses. How they figured that would be enough against all the Indians in the valley, she didn't know. But then, the mind of men like Bates had never been easy to unravel. They seemed not to care how much carnage they sowed. They seemed impervious to the bloodshed and disunity they created.

Jessie couldn't reconcile with that. All she'd ever sought was to be left in peace, free to live her life and to let others live theirs, content with what they had and happy to share around what extra there was. Bates and his kind were insatiable.

The trail led her in a long winding pursuit. They clearly did not know where to find the people they sought. The soft haze of late afternoon was filling the coulees and gullies by the time she came close.

The men had stopped in a small valley. They stood about, their horses off to one side, grazing, and Bates was letting rip. Apparently, something was not going according to his liking.

Jessie dismounted, slung her saddlebags over her shoulder, and crept closer, listening to his ranting.

"I swear, Jeff, if you're double-crossing me, I'll make sure you get your neck stretched. I'm askin' you one last time. Is this where the Indians camped or not?"

Jessie lay on her belly beneath a clump of large sagebrush, watching the men below. Bates looked incensed. Jeff looked sullen. The others, the big Irishman and another man Jessie didn't know, were looking a mite confused, even a bit put out, by Bates's behavior.

Rafe stood close to Bates, his face deadpan. On the opposite side of Bates stood Ned Wilson, his hand on his pistol butt. Probably the reason Bates felt safe enough to pile into folks like they were kids he'd caught with their hands in the cookie jar.

"I know it don't look like it, but I swear they were here," Jeff Walters insisted. "What does it matter? We just—"

Bates didn't let him finish his sentence. "What does it matter? You all-fired no-account cowpoke! It matters when we're huntin' down thieves and murderers! If you don't think it matters, what in tarnation are you doin' here?"

Walters scowled. "So let's get to huntin' them, then."

Bates bristled. "I don't like the sound of your tone, Walters!" he snapped.

"Now just hold up right there, Bates," Sonny Blaine cut in, stepping up to stand beside Jeff Walters. "You ain't our schoolmarm, but you sure sound like one. If you want us to stick by you on this, you'd better quit playin' the landlord and treat us like we're your equals."

Jessie took her cue. Before Bates could open his mouth to retort, she strode into the center of the gathering. Bates coughed and nearly choked as she looked him squarely in the eye. Rafe tensed up, and his hand quivered near his Colt.

Bates shot him a venomous glare, which Rafe instantly reflected onto Jessie. She ignored them, focusing instead on the other men. Walters, Blaine, Crawford.

"Howdy fellas," she said, pulling out the maps and title deeds she'd found in Bates's study and laying them out on the ground. "I reckon I got me a notion why Bates would play the landlord. Likely because he reckons he is the landlord, or he will be right soon."

"What are you talking about, Jessie?" Sonny came closer, peering at one map.

"Oh, I'll just make it easy an' read this sweet little love letter from a Mr. Hastings to our friend Bates," Jessie replied. She pulled the letter from her pocket and unfolded it, staring Bates right in the face. He looked like he was about to explode. Jessie didn't care. If he or Rafe took a notion to shoot her in front of so many witnesses, they'd have more explaining to do than they knew how.

She gave him a little smile, inclined her head, cleared her throat, and read. With every damning word that came out of her mouth, the surrounding atmosphere grew thicker. The ranchers stared at Bates in shock and disbelief. Everyone, except Crawford, Rafe, and Wilson. Their faces were darkening at the same rate as Bates's. They clearly had their fingers in the pie, too.

When she finished the letter, reading off the name of the sender, she looked around at the stunned men. "Oh, and by the by, if any of you fellas feel a hankerin' to meet the charmin' Mr. Hastings, he's tied up in Frenchie's old cabin, if you know where that is.

Bates cussed violently and gripped his pistol butt. At the same moment, Sonny drew his own weapon and leveled it at the rancher.

"You twitch so much as an eyelid, Gale Bates, and I'll put a round or six of lead into you. The judge won't mind. Cattle rustlin' and horse thievin' both count for a hangin' anyhow."

Bates lifted his hands away from his sides in a show of surrender, but his eyes, boring into Jessie's, were full of hatred. It didn't bother her too much and it wasn't the first time someone like Bates had given her such a look. And it likely wouldn't be the last. All she cared about was that her mission had succeeded.

At last, the real cattle thief had been branded.

Chapter 14
Goodbyes

Jessie sat on the large boulder that served as Danny's headstone and stared out over the French homestead below. It lay peacefully under the midmorning sun. A gentle breeze ruffled the leaves of the pines and cottonwoods around her and toyed with the smoke rising from the cabin chimney.

"You should've seen Sonny Blaine an' Jeff Walters rollin' this here stone over your grave, Danny," she said out loud. It comforted her to speak to Danny loud enough so she could hear herself instead of just in her mind. "You never seen fellas heave and shove so hard. Made me feel right weepy, them goin' like all get out, as if they wanted t' make it up to you they'd ever gone along with Rafe and Bates and their schemes."

She paused, blinking back the tears, blurring her vision.

"Tanner lent a hand, too. He don't say much, but I can see he misses you, too, Dan. You were a good friend to him, like he's been a good friend to the both of us."

Jessie stopped. A rider was coming up the hillside toward her. It was the very man she'd just been speaking of. She knew what he was coming to tell her.

On the one hand, she didn't want to know. On the other, it might just settle something in her. She watched Tanner ride up to the boulder, ground-tether his horse, and clamber up onto the rock beside her.

He sat silently for a while, and Jessie knew he was respecting her solitude and sorrow. She hadn't had time to mourn the loss of her brother, what with all the shenanigans that followed his murder.

Jessie closed her eyes and felt the wind caressing her cheek, playing with her bandanna. It was a comfort to have Tanner nearby, even though he wasn't saying anything.

At last, she opened her eyes and turned her head to look at him. "The trial's over then, is it?" she asked.

"Yeah," Tanner breathed out with a sigh. He kept staring at the homestead below, or the mountains beyond. Jessie wasn't quite sure.

"You goin' t' tell me about it, or must I drag it out of ya?" Jessie said, giving her friend a dig in the ribs with her elbow.

Tanner looked over at her, his eyes a little haunted. Then he seemed to relax and gave her a smile. "You'll be happy t' know the judge booked 'em all in at the Crowbar Hotel," Tanner said with a lopsided grin, the haunted look still casting a pale shadow across his eyes.

"All? How many were in on the deal with Hastings?" Jessie hoped it wouldn't be too many of the ranchers. Most of them had struck her as being pretty good folks, just easily misled by self-confident, loud types like Bates.

"Just Rafe and that Wilson fella from the fort. Crawford was in on it, too, but he got off with a big fine. I reckon he'll have to sell nigh on all his stock just t' pay it off."

Jessie nodded and looked away. Just as well they'd never gone to work for that man. They might not have got as far as they did in exposing Bates and his lies. "How about the others? How'd they take it?"

Tanner chuckled wryly. "Well, I got me a notion that wise old judge put Hastings and Bates away to keep 'em safe from big ol' Sonny Blaine. He was steamin' at the ears, I tell ya. More than ready to knock Bates's block off if they had given him half a chance. Nobody likes to be taken for a fool. Sonny Blaine least of all."

"They get everybody's cows back?"

"Yeah. Rafe up and 'fessed they hid them in a canyon five or six miles from the Bates homestead. The boys are drivin' 'em back to their rightful owners right this minute."

"You didn't go with 'em?"

"Frenchie said I should come tell you how things were shakin' out. We figured you'd want to know." He looked away as he spoke, but Jessie could hear his voice break a little. Then he turned back to face her again. "I spoke to the judge, Jess. He said he's happy t' open up Danny's case again. Do a proper inquest." His eyes searched hers.

Jessie looked away and shook her head. "Naw. Won't do him any good now, anyhow. Nor me, come t' think of it. Our Dan never was the vengeful kind, and if they find Rafe guilty, he'll hang sure as a gun. I can only hope he'll mend his ways. If he don't, he'll get what's comin' to him."

She was silent for a while, and they both sat listening to the whisper of the wind and the cry of a kite. The memory of that day her brother had saved her life by giving his own played out before her mind's eye like she was seeing it for the first time.

"You know, Tanner, I was thinkin' about Danny jumpin' in front of Rafe's gun. That's one of the purest things I've seen a fella do. It's a kind of love few folks have. Layin' down their life in place of someone else's. I reckon it won't do t' stain that memory with a heap of long, drawn-out inquests and trials."

"That's God's honest truth," Tanner agreed, his voice once again sounding choked up.

For a long time after that, they sat silent. Jessie felt a little surprised she didn't feel the need for him to leave her alone again. The old Jessie would have wanted to be on her own, but now it seemed like the most natural thing in the world to have Tanner there, his voiceless presence as tangible as the wind tousling her hair and the solid rock supporting her.

Down below, she could see Tasha walking out of the cabin with Macawi on her hip. Chaske skipped along at her side, swinging his arms and looking up at his mother now and then. Jessie could imagine him babbling away to her about something or other.

Frenchie was riding up the trail toward his home, accompanied by Wally and some other cowhands, driving a packet of at least fifty cows. It was a joyful sight that signaled the end of a chapter in Jessie's life that she didn't want to reread any time soon.

"Looks like it's about grub time," Tanner said awkwardly.

Jessie nodded.

"You hungry?"

"Not much," Jessie said. "You go on ahead. I think I'll just sit a little longer."

"Suit yourself," Tanner replied. Then he coughed. "You thought on what to do next?"

It was a question Jessie had been asking herself a lot in the last few hours. She wasn't entirely sure she had the answer yet. "Yeah, I thought on it. Can't say I've decided one way or another. One thing I know, I can't stay here at Crazy Woman Canyon no more. Too many memories I'd rather forget."

"Frenchie an' Tasha'll sure miss ya. Little Chaske, too."

Jessie sighed, vaguely wondering why Tanner didn't include himself on that list. "Yeah. Reckon I'll miss them, too. But there it is. Life don't always turn out the way we want it to."

In that moment, she knew what she was going to do. "Reckon I came up here t' say goodbye t' Danny. Soon as I feel like I'm done, I'll be hittin' the trail."

Tanner shifted his seat. "Any idea where you'll be headin'?"

"Naw. I reckon I'll know when I get there." It was true. She had no plans. Drifting felt like an almighty welcome idea.

"I figured as much," Tanner said. Another long silence passed, which Tanner broke once more. "You reckon you'll mind some company taggin' along?"

Jessie looked over at her friend. Funny, she'd been hoping he'd say that. "Can't say I will, if it's you that's offerin'," she replied with a grin. "An' I know you an' me both will always have Danny with us. In our hearts, anyhow."

Tanner smiled back, the haunted look in his eyes suddenly gone. Jessie leaned over and rested her head against his shoulder, all at once feeling tired right down into her bones.

She heard Tanner suck in his breath. It was understandable. She'd surprised herself, letting him that close.

Without a word, Tanner encircled her shoulders with one arm. Jessie closed her eyes and didn't shrug it off. She didn't have to wonder why. She couldn't remember ever feeling as safe as she did in that moment.

The End

I hope you enjoyed this story. If so, I would appreciate a positive review on Amazon.

More Westerns are in the works...coming soon.

www.ingramcontent.com/pod-product-compliance
Lightning Source LLC
Chambersburg PA
CBHW052012150726
47999CB00004B/1623